The Half-Life of Songs

The Half-Life *of* Songs

DAVID GAFFNEY

LONDON

PUBLISHED BY SALT PUBLISHING
Dutch House, 307–308 High Holborn, London WC1V 7LL United Kingdom

© David Gaffney, 2010

Printed and bound in Great Britain by
CPI Antony Rowe, Chippenham and Eastbourne

Typeset in Paperback 10/14

ISBN 978 1 84471 775 0 paperback

1 3 5 7 9 8 6 4 2

for Hannah and Sarah

Contents

HALF OPEN

A Certain Type of Man

THE RECESSION PUSHED the four barbers into reviewing their set up costs and it was Jamie who suggested they cancel the new sign, which was going to cost five hundred quid.

'What? And leave the name of the last shop up there?' said Steve.

'The Lingerie Lounge?' moaned Alf.

'Why not?' said Charley, who had returned with a box of doughnuts he proceeded to pass round. 'It would be funny.'

'After all,' put in Steve, his mouth full of jam, 'we are all comfortable with our sexuality, are we not?'

'Yes,' the four barbers said in one deep voice.

The customers of Widnes didn't care that the new barbershop was called the Lingerie Lounge. A clipper cut and a few grunts about the football and seventies rock was all they wanted. So the four barbers went further. A number two became a two denier, those thinning on top got a peephole bra cut, and the bloke with the strip of hair down the centre got a thong.

'What about we start wearing things,' Alf said one day.

'What sort of things?' said Steve.

'You know. Bras and stuff. Just on a Saturday, like. We wouldn't want it to look weird.'

So, each Saturday the four middle-aged large-bellied

ex-chemical workers wore an assortment of complicated ladies underwear over their checked shirts and jeans: slinky and rhinestone, sheer and leopard-print, whore-red and black lacey. Customers loved it and business rocketed. Ron Farrer the barber down the road couldn't compete. He was a lone operator and it would have looked a bit odd if he took to dressing up.

It wasn't until a man came over the bridge from Runcorn and asked if his daughter could wait while he had a four denier on the sides and a fun-fur open crotch on the top that the four barbers decided the original shop title, PJ Kelly and Partners, might be worth the extra money.

Talking About
Emmy-Lou

BORIS WAS TESTING different styles of bootlace tie against Nigel's shirt when he noticed the new ruby collar-tips. They hadn't come from Boris's shop so Boris asked Nigel where he'd got them.

Nigel was shifty. 'You know, Boris, I'm not bothered by what you said about Emmy-Lou. Country is a broad church. I'm not part of any boycott.'

Nigel seemed like a good guy, but there was something odd about the ruby collar-tips. Cowboy Clobber was the only shop in Heywood for western paraphernalia and Boris would be surprised if Nigel had been shopping elsewhere. Nigel considered an unfamiliar supermarket an adventure and was too stuck in his ways to tap his Visa number into the internet.

'New buttons as well, Nige?'

'I got them off the indoor market.'

The old lady kept her buttons in long transparent tubes with a sample of each button on the end. It was a good system, reminded him of a sweet shop.

Boris picked up a few buttons from a loose collection

in a basket and let them fall through his fingers as the old woman watched him. The market stunk of Spam muffins.

'You got any Western-type stuff?' he said after a time. 'Like, you know, cowboy?'

The old woman looked about the market and then hooked a finger at him, drawing him in close.

'I have a few things,' she said, and from somewhere pulled out a big catalogue and flipped the pages fast in front of his eyes. Diamante iron-ons, gambler coats, and cowhide spectacle cases flashed past.

'What about the shop on the high street,' Boris said, 'doesn't he sell all the cowboy stuff round here?'

'Yes. But since the Emmy-Lou thing people don't like to go in there so much. Soft rock?' she hissed in a disgusted tone. 'Emmy-Lou is Country through and through. If that man said that about Emmy-Lou, what else is he going to say? If Emmy is soft rock then Jones never took the ride-on mower down the pub. Me and my husband fell in love to "Desperado".'

The old woman's eyes were deep-set and small, like the tiniest of the buttons she sold, and they shone with tears.

'I can get you any Western-themed item you desire,' she said. 'This company,' she tapped the catalogue, 'they have a van.'

Everything's Gone Turquoise

THE CATHOLIC CENTRE had plenty of Guinness, an accordionist who played a hi-hat with his foot, and a shiny floor for the kids to slide about on in their socks. But everyone was hungry after marching through town wearing shamrock hats and tooting kazoos and no one had thought to put on food.

'The Guinness is lying heavy on these fellahs.' It was Eileen Monahan, his new mother-in-law. 'Get as much as you can. And meat, mind, none of that caterpillar shite.' She pushed a fat roll of twenties into Dempsey's hand. 'And make sure it's Irish-themed.'

Dempsey looked at Eileen's glitter-studded white flares and emerald Stetson.

'Exactly, Dempsey,' she said. 'Loosen up, buoy.'

Snow was falling and the wind sent daggers through Dempsey's shirt; where to get food for a party of 300 on a Sunday afternoon with Greggs shut?

He found his man outside the butcher's, in a green coat and white hat, calling 'all chickens a pound'.

Dempsey showed the man the roll of notes. 'How many for that?'

The butcher looked at the wad, then at his watch. Then

he went inside and wrapped two hundred cooked chickens in a cloth and loaded them onto a trolley. They smelt like the heated-up dripping from a thousand old pans.

'Oh, and I need them to be Irish themed,' Dempsey said.

The butcher took off his cap. Snowflakes settled and melted on his bald head.

'Well, you could dye them,' he said, then looked across at the dark windows of Woolworth's, shut down for the last 6 months. 'But I'm not sure where you'd get the colour. Try Mellow Moments.'

In Mellow Moments there was a steel-booted Goth with holes in her earlobes a bee could fly through. She sold him a tub of bath crystals which would turn the chickens green and was flavourless and safe to eat.

The men at the Catholic Centre roared at the pyramid of turquoise chickens, and Tom Flynn picked up a chicken and danced with it, gripping its stumpy leg in his hand and stroking its back. But when he saw the turquoise dye all over his shirt he drop-kicked the chicken into the air and this inspired everyone to storm in and grab at the chickens and soon men, children and cooked chickens were skidding everywhere, and everything was turning turquoise. One fellah jammed a chicken on top of the accordionist's hi hat, and as Dempsey headed for the fire exit, he saw the turquoise chicken going up and down on the off-beat of 'Forty Shades of Green', and heard Eileen Monahan calling, 'Dempsey? Where's Dempsey? Has anyone seen Dempsey?'

The History Brush

'When you live here, in Eggborough,' Mr Fuller said, 'you don't even see the towers. It's as if the towers aren't there. They are not there to all intents and purposes. I mean they are there, but they're not. Not really. I accept that when an outsider sees a house in Eggborough they notice the big fuck-off power plant with eight huge cooling towers in the background. But that's not what Eggborough people see. They see the sky. So what I am asking you to do is to help me to produce a more accurate visual representation of how the houses in Eggborough would look if you actually lived here.'

I showed Mr Fuller how you could use the history brush to wipe over the towers and replace them with blue sky.

'Excellent,' Mr Fuller said.

'How about I add something?' I said.

'What were you thinking of?'

'I was thinking of a rainbow.'

Mr Fuller went to the window and looked out. 'I've seen rainbows in Eggborough. It's possible. It wouldn't be a lie. But doesn't that mean it's been raining? No one wants to buy a wet house.'

'You can have a rainbow in a blue sky,' I said, 'look,' and I showed him what I'd done: liquid ribbons of colour, shimmering.

9

I enjoyed replacing the towers with rainbows, but after a few weeks got bored and began to add unicorns as well, hidden in the dappled shadows of lawns. You could hardly see them, but I knew they were there, and every time I sneaked a unicorn into one of the photos, that house sold quicker than any of the others. I didn't tell Mr Fuller. He was a practical man who liked to believe his achievements were down to human ingenuity; magic had no place in the story of Mr Fuller's success.

Having it Like Pontefract

T**HE FELLAH ASKED** if he could take a photograph of Randolph's sweets and Randolph was already pissed off because the bloke who'd imported the Slovakian Brylcreem had been cleaning up and leaving the rest of them without a sniff, so he told the fellah to fuck off. Why would he want photographs of Randolph's sweets? Be more helpful if he bought some. People are supposed to buy more sweets in a recession, but Randolph hadn't seen any signs of that. Later he saw the same fellah again, taking photographs of the onion-bagging machine behind the vegetable shop, so he got Moira to mind the stall and went straight down to Citizens Advice to see what they could tell him about his rights. But when he got there, there was no receptionist any more, just a door buzzer in the foyer. He pushed it, but nothing happened.

A woman was pacing up and down the foyer and he asked her how long she'd been waiting and if she'd pushed the buzzer, but she just rolled her eyes at him.

Randolph tried again, jamming his thumb hard against the button for several seconds. He couldn't hear anything but guessed that the buzzer was a long way away, deep inside. He stared through the glass doors down a long corridor.

'If you can't get someone to answer a buzzer,' he said to the woman, 'where are your rights?'

'They'll have it like Pontefract,' she said

'They want it like Pontefract,' Randolph said. 'That's the problem.'

He pressed the buzzer again and put his ear against the glass and from somewhere deep within Citizens Advice he thought he heard a chair scrape.

HALF AWARE

Towns in France Exactly Like This

A NAKED TWENTY-TWO-year-old French girl stood somewhere above Gary's head. Mademoiselle Pelletier arrived every Tuesday at half-past-six; pink sunglasses on her face, floppy velvet hat on her head, cigarette cocked in her hand, long Afghan coat obscuring her feet so she seemed to glide up the staircase on a jet of air. Gary snapped shut his acetylene torch and flipped up his visor to watch her go by. The art students — speccy, pencil-necked twonks who didn't deserve to see a fully-clothed French woman, never mind a naked one —followed later, a solemn hush falling about them as they ascended to the art room. Gary stood by his pipe-work and imagined the young French model above him disporting her straggly goatskin and striking her pose by the whirring fan heater. One evening he snatched a student's drawing, but the smudgy charcoal representation of Mademoiselle Pelletier's nakedness disappointed; how could this teenaged hippy in John Lennon specs capture her delirious Gallic beauty?

Three packets of fags and a bottle of Bacardi persuaded Roy the caretaker to let Gary into the roof space, and that

Tuesday, Roy and Gary lay above the humming fan heater, muggy air blowing up into their faces, looking down through the ventilation grids as art teacher, Mr. Donald, smoked a cigarette and waited.

At half-past-six, Mademoiselle Pelletier appeared; the floppy velvet hat sailed off and her long caramel hair fanned out, sparkling in the electric light. She called out hello to Mr Donald, her voice brittle and quavery, the way a dragonfly might speak, and Mr. Donald suggested she make herself comfortable, turning away quickly to occupy himself with arranging pencils. Mademoiselle Pelletier glanced at his hunched back, a quizzical, comical expression on her face, then she kicked off her cracked magnolia moccasins, chucked her Afghan coat onto a chair, shrugged off her raggedy cheesecloth blouse, unhitched the snake buckle of her belt, allowing her long elephant-belled jeans to slide down her legs, and suddenly she had departed the world of clothing and entered a world of flesh.

She was thin. Gary wanted to take her home — to fatten her, to spoil her, to nuzzle his face in her hair while she stroked his head and scolded him in her wispy French voice. She had small, uptilted breasts that seemed to want to fly up towards the ceiling like trembling birds and they quivered as she bent to pick up her dressing gown. Gary allowed a sigh to escape from his lips and Roy elbowed him hard.

Mr. Donald helped Mademoiselle Pelletier into her dressing gown and the twenty-two-year-old naked French girl and the tweedy middle-aged teacher sat down together and lit cigarettes and talked quietly as if in a church, her tiny voice flittering around Mr. Donald's long, mooing vowels. They covered many subjects: the volume of traffic in the town and the new ring road, the town's poor facilities and how dull the place must be for a French girl. He wasn't to worry, she said, there were towns in France exactly like this. They discussed a play at the local theatre and what drugs you could get in the town's more way-out pubs and how terrible it was that some young people nowadays took drugs, but how you could understand it when there was nothing to do in a town like this. They talked about Neil Young and Carole King. Mr. Donald's son had seen Hawkwind and they had a naked girl dancer and a bubble machine. Did she know the dancer? No. She didn't know the bubble machine either.

The art students filed in, coughing edgily and taking furtive looks at Mm Pelletier while pretending to be busy with their artist's accoutrements. Easels were positioned, pencils sharpened and Mme Pelletier stood. Her robe fell and after a few seconds of astonished silence, pencils began to screak screak screak like grasshopper legs, and Gary and Roy shifted their positions to get a better view though the petal-holes in the metal grill. Mr Donald switched a radio on and John Peel was playing Pink Floyd's 'Wish You Were Here', an aching guitar figure of four dissonant chiming twangs. Gary believed that there was no place better to be in 1975 than lying in the dark above a fan heater listening to Pink Floyd and looking at a naked French girl. This was what Gary was thinking when the groaning sound began from the joists near his elbow. The groan became a squeak and then a rasp, and then a long whine of steel nails twisting and tearing out from their fixings. The world tilted up and suddenly Gary was on top of Mm Pelletier and Roy was on top of Mr. Donald. Gary leapt up from Mm Pelletier and as she looked down at her nakedness, she noticed a little Pollock-splat of blood seeping from a scratch on her wrist.

'Oh, no,' she said in her little voice, 'there's a notch!' and she turned her eyes to Gary and the eyes were green and flecked with pearls of grey that floated like clouds and he saw a miniature city in those clouds and bought a house in that city, and in that house lived happily for the rest of his life with Mm Pelletier, and all this happened in a space of nine seconds.

Gary told his dad it didn't matter that he'd been expelled because he wasn't interested in plumbing anymore, he wanted to be an artist and draw French girls. But his dad said that art was for poofs and any sensible French girl would rather shag a plumber. The French are a practical, logical race, he explained. They have many large fields, homes miles from mains utilities, and five times as many septic tanks as the rest of the world.

The phone was answered by the thin voice of a dragonfly and she put her father on who agreed to Gary's quote for the new sink right away.

The Pelletier family were out for the day, so there was plenty of time for Gary to install the sink in the way he wanted, and without interference. The job required many different thicknesses of pipe, but once he'd assembled them, it was easy to weld the metal tubes together into the collection of shapes that was burnt into his memory. Mains drainage pipes were good for her thighs, and delicately braided overflow pipes formed her arms. The trembling birds of her breasts were miniature metal washbasins welded to her cistern chest. For the face he used copper straws looped over and over to build up that quizzical, comical expression that had stayed with him over the years. The structure worked too — the water came in at one end, passed through Mademoiselle Pelletier's naked body, and ended up in the sink.

Mademoiselle Pelletier would recognise her naked self right away. Pipe-work is a creative endeavour, you can get real emotion into it. The only feature that might concern her was the eyes. The eyes in his pipe sculpture were an absence, an expression of loss, the black holes that had sucked Gary's soul into this abyss, this endless span of wanting, yearning, of eternally being without her.

Junctions One to Four Were Never Built

MARY LIT THE candle and breathed in its scent. Then she looked out of the window and there it was: the graceful curve of a motorway, arcing up over the roof-tops like a gleaming, futuristic monorail. A motorway that wasn't there. She remembered the planner's diagrams, the consultation documents everyone had responded to with a resounding no. Not Mary. Mary wanted it. She wanted its speed, its urgency. The motorway's route was burned deep into the topography of Mary's mind. This section of motorway existed for her. She imagined the tramps that hung about under its flyovers, the kids that graffitied its giant posts and bridges.

Peacocks put out a product recall on the candles. They had been alerted to the effects by a woman in Warrington who had lit one and immediately seen a huge factory at the bottom of her garden, a factory she knew had never been built. But Mary didn't want to take her candles back. She lit one every night and every night she breathed its scent and every night she saw the motorway again. Outside her door was junction three. If she concentrated, she could hear the hiss of tires as a river of invisible metal ran towards the docks. Something bricked up inside her had been released.

Buildings Crying Out

N<small>O ONE KNEW</small> where Harold came from. The tunnel was discovered later. He would appear at unpredictable times and offer to help, and Pauline seemed happy with his contributions, so she gave him jobs and didn't worry about his legitimacy as a worker, or indeed whether anyone ever paid him. The museum was a liberal place; staff members had been in various lefty organisations, in the days when long-haired people joined things, thought about things, and cared about things other than recycling cartons.

Harold had strange habits. I watched him one day walking up and down a particular section of floor, lifting his feet like a show pony, his head cocked to the side, listening. Later I saw him with his head against a filing cabinet, sliding the drawers in and out, relishing the vibrations of the rolling bearings, the crisp clink of the runners hitting the safety stopper.

Harold was interested in the noises a building made. He would listen for the way sounds coaxed other sounds from the building—echoes of themselves, or sympathetic cries from other objects, such as a vase shuddering at a passing train, or the way when a particular chair was scraped across a certain section of floor it created a harmonic that triggered a pane of glass in another room to give off a plaintiff whine, which was an exact sixth harmony to the original note of the chair scrape, and he would explain to whoever was close that this was related to air currents, temperature and humidity, and happened only in a very particular set of circumstances and we were very lucky to hear it.

We couldn't hear it, if we were honest. But we humoured him. It was Harold's indestructible belief that every sound in a building should work with every other, a choir of clerical ticks and murmurs. We wondered if he was about to invent a job for himself—a sound policeman, who would tune the zips on our anoraks and instruct us on the correct way to rustle paper. We knew one thing for certain: he was especially interested in the sound of closing doors.

It was no surprise to me when one day I heard a commotion from the foyer and went down to find Pauline arguing with a couple of prisons officers.

I knew right away who they were looking for and found Harold with his head against a Sellotape dispenser listening to its trundle mechanism. He told me all about the tunnel and why he'd been leaving the prison and coming here every day.

The judge had said there was only one way to change Harold. He needed to hear a special sound. A clang. The Clang. The clang of a prison door. Harold told me how he had sat in the security van and imagined the power of the clang that awaited him. An iron thunderclap, like a giant foundry press that shakes a whole town. But when it came time for Harold's cell door to be closed and he made himself ready for that terrible clang, he was disappointed. The locks were computerised and his door closed with the fairy metallic whisper of shifting pins and a soft electric squelch. This sound would never change a man.

I imagined him being led down long, swallowing

corridors back to his clean modern cell where he would lie and listen carefully to the prison officer's retreating footsteps till the sound died away to nothing and there was nothing left to hear. Later that night, I pictured him lying awake, listening to the sounds the prison made. Not the cacophony of squawks and moans from the prisoners, but the cries of the building itself as people tried to live inside it.

Everlast

KATHLEEN PRESSED HER face against the glass. An inch from her eye, in viscous, green fluid, Pete Doherty's pale fingers were curled into a claw, as if forming a final chord. This was the hand, the very hand, that tugged her through London streets to a terraced house for a secret gig the police broke up after three songs.

She rocked the case and a tiny hair on Doherty's knuckle trembled.

Why did it have to be like this?

She looked at the other case, where the rest of Doherty was suspended. His corpse had been sliced vertically down the middle, both eyes staring straight ahead forever. Kathleen wondered if his soul might have been happier had the cases been arranged the other way round — at least one eye would be looking towards the rest of his body.

She threw her arms out sideways and touched both cases, drawing breath sharply. Pete Doherty's body. She was standing between the two halves of Doherty, almost inside him, the closest she'd been to the man, and the only time she'd seen him naked.

His heart looked like any heart, his liver too. His intestines were red, like anybody's, his kidneys brownish. His skin looked perfect — the many pockmarks and bruises gone. Why was this perfect body not alive? Surely they could stitch the halves together, throw some electricity through him and jolt him back to life? Back to the Doherty we'd loved — the tipped trilby, the torn T-shirt, the eyeliner.

But this was what Doherty had specified. Some left their bodies to science; Doherty left his to art.

One arm had been arranged to trail down in the manner, the artist stated on the interpretation panel, of The Death of Chatterton by Henry Wallis. Around the room, other figures lay in the same Chatterton pose: the same purple-blue silk breeches, the same window half open, the same curtain moving in the breeze, the same burnt-out candle with its smoke curling up, the same single fading rose, petals dripping onto the window ledge. Curtis, Cobain, Hendrix, Presley — the list went on.

Tonight had been the private view and it had been easy to hide whilst the other guests went home. Kathleen needed one last kiss — formaldehyde or no formaldehyde. The hammer was designed to break safety glass and it worked — each blow shattered another layer and soon vile vapour seeped from the cracks making her sneeze, gasp, then double-up coughing as though she might retch herself inside out. But she went on until the glass case collapsed and Doherty's carcass flopped onto the floor like a sodden roll of carpet. She fell upon him, gripped his hair and lifted his half-head towards her lips. Chemicals scorched her skin, and the knives in her heart were not love. She felt a violent shivering fit, a pounding in her ears flooding her brain and all the way to her toes and fingertips. Something brown throbbed behind her eyes.

Chatterton, looking down from the wall, seemed to disapprove, and Kathleen tried with her last gasp to arrange her arm in a way he might like, and she thought, as her eyes closed for the last time, that she'd not done a bad job.

The Forcing of Air

CLECKHEATON ACCORDION SHOP was the centre of the world when it came to accordion-based master class DVDs, and Russell, a young virtuoso who had toured with Sharon Shannon, was the perfect choice to make a version for melodeon players.

But the owner of Cleckheaton accordion shop had been watching the rushes, and wasn't happy with one of the sections.

'Was it the bit where I dangled the box on its side and played an A-run on the pull, with the bellows opening with the force of gravity?' Russell said.

'I liked that bit,' the owner said. 'That was fine.'

'Was it the bit where I tap triplets on a single button using three different fingers?'

'That worked fine as well,' the owner said.

'The bit where I showed them how to play in B on a D/G box?'

'No, no. It was,' the owner passed his hand through the air as if catching something intangible, 'all the other stuff. At the end.'

Ever since he was young, Russell had been fascinated by accordions, squeeze boxes and melodeons. He couldn't believe where the raucous sound came from. His mother told him little elves were trapped inside, mad for the taste of light and air, and every time you opened the bellows, you allowed everyone to hear the elves crying out.

Russell took to the melodeon like a natural and each time he played he thought about the elves. He began to think about the elves even when he wasn't playing. He worried about them, stuck inside the dark bellows, huddled in corners weeping quietly, or laughing manically, in a silent world where no one could hear them until Russell began to play.

As a teenager, he wanted to make the elves scream, make their little voices leap up in pain. He wanted to make them work faster and harder than they ever had before. Sometimes he felt violent. His mates had their thrash-metal and would writhe on the floor, shaking their hair to grinding riffs, while Russell took his adolescent frustration out on the melodeon. The box was a throat he was squeezing, its bellows folds of skin that hinged the joints of some cruel monster.

So, at the end of the film, Russell looked straight into the camera and told the viewers about the elves crying out from their dark prison in the folds and how it was the player's job to make these elves sing; to coax them, to thrill them, to seduce them, torture them, even.

The owner of Cleckheaton accordion shop wasn't so impressed with this last part.

'How about,' he suggested, 'if you just said thanks for watching and good luck with your playing?'

Live Feed

THE PUB WAS packed and dozens of people had spilled into the garden where the landlord had placed an extra screen so no one would miss a thing.

Jack couldn't see what was wrong with watching in private at home.

Community spirit, mob mentality.

'Looking forward to the show, Jack?' It was Jimmy Mcloughlin, chair of the Chorlton-on-Medlock Watercolour Society.

'I am, Jimmy,' said Jack.

'Gonna be tense in there. A lot of rivalries been simmering.' Jimmy had a crazy, feral streak, and lacked the normal human aversion to physical violence. Events like this were an excuse to vent the fury he brewed all year. 'See you inside?'

'Yeh, I'll see you in there,' said Jack. 'But Jimmy — it's only art, remember?'

Jimmy smiled, shook his head and disappeared into the enclosing crowd.

Jack wished he was actually there, at the exhibition. As usual, he was policing the live coverage in the community.

'It's your excellent people-skills,' DCI Rogers explained. 'The people trust you, Jack. You have the ability to avoid taking sides, and we don't all have that. You understand the issues, but don't get worked up.'

That might be true, but Jack would still rather be there, with the star artists, the celebrities — the Prime Minister, for Christ's sake. At the actual event it was much easier to control the disorder that always went with these big exhibitions. The Velasquez in Birmingham, the Monet in Sheffield, the Titian in Liverpool, they all ended up the same. Bloodbaths. At the actual event you were in a controlled environment and could use your baton, your cuffs, and sometimes, if you got the go ahead, gas and water cannon. It had been known. Kandinsky at Leeds, for example. Two dead, dozens injured. At Klimt they had gone mental. Jack had no reason to believe that this latest blockbuster would be any different.

Here, at the White Swan in Fallowfield, he'd get to have a few friendly words with the so-called community leaders who would calm things down a little if Jack was lucky, but if anything serious kicked off it could end up with him calling for backup. And how did that make him look? Still, he wouldn't ring right way. He'd let them have their head. There were advantages to being at the heart of the trouble. He patted the bulge in his inside pocket. When it all kicked off and no one was watching, Jack would get an opportunity to practice his own art.

He looked across the pub to where the Italian supporters were sat. Next to them, the Pre-Raphaelite brigade, then the photography lot, then the grassroots mob from the smaller schools and provincial galleries. The grassroots were the worst. Jimmy's bunch, the Chorlton-on-Medlock Watercolour Society, were notoriously vicious. Yet the hard core had been flushed out long ago. Guns were off the scene, and the violence had become ritualised — balletic, almost.

Their neat, quick razors spritzed up blood up in a fine spray, making things look much worse than the actual wounds inflicted. The fighting was ceremonial and had gathered around itself a beauty of its own, a quality it seemed to draw from the art.

The screen flickered and soon the camera was off, tracking along the main exhibits. Paintings floated by and at each one an ooo or aah was exhaled by the dazzled viewers. Then the camera came to the decorative art section and stopped on the Italian Sgabello chair.

Jimmy McLoughlin leapt up. 'A chair? A fucking chair? How exactly is that art? If I want to look at a chair, I'll visit World of fucking Leather. Get this shite off our screens.'

Bedlam broke out. The fight started in the pub, but quickly spilled over into the garden and the street. Jack watched from the edge, his hand from time to time drifting towards his pocket. There were occasions when he thought he might need backup. But eventually the rioters got tired and the fighting relaxed into a drowsy punch-up, as if underwater.

Jack spoke to Jimmy before they grabbed him. 'Come on, Jimmy. You could stop this if you wanted to. You have influence. It's only art, after all.'

'Only art,' Jimmy said. 'For Christ's sake, Jack, your problem is you don't feel it. You know the names of the artists, you know their history, you can name the major exhibitions, all the movements, you've got it all pat. You can pass that off in the pub. But you don't feel it here. That's what this is all about.' He waved his hand towards the knots of scuffling bodies, the burning cars, the shattered shop windows, the tongues of flame from petrol bombs. 'Passion, it's called.'

The Pre-Raphaelites dragged Jimmy down a ginnel and

Jack followed close behind. He didn't intervene. Jimmy wouldn't have wanted him to. In the dim light of the ginnel, Jack saw the glint of the blade as they held him down. He took out his camera and began to film. He had a live feed to dozens of galleries, arts centres and museums all over the country. There would be cheers as the close-up of Jimmy's face filled the screens, and screams of delight when the blade slipped across his stubbly face, delicate feathers of crimson flicking up. This was what discerning art lovers wanted, this was art at its highest, with real emotions and real people, an art form few understood, but for those who did, was the highest of all, and Jack, a pioneer.

HALF THERE

The Three Daves

F AT DAVE THOUGHT Budapest was shabby-chic.
Little Dave thought Paris was shoe-shop-manager-on-a-midlife crisis. Big Dave didn't want a repeat of Krakow where they had to put on padded clothing and get chased through the woods by attack dogs. So, for a laugh, Big Dave suggested they have the stag in Pontefract, where they'd visited the liquorish museum as part of a confectionary campaign. Little Dave said yes right away, and Fat Dave loved the idea. It would be uber-post-post-ironic-out-the-other-side-and-back-into-being-just-ironic. Shoreditch media spods in sarcastically tilted flat caps sipping mini-Bollingers in the street. There was even a Wimpy, so they could eat burgers off a plate with a knife and fork. It was Little Dave's idea to use the stone troughs in the market place, and the president of the Metropolitan Drinking Fountain and Cattle Trough Association was so impressed that Pontrefract's troughs would be returned to something like their original use that he gave his blessing right away.

The night before the stag, the three Daves donned overalls and went into the town to prepare their troughs. Each Dave had a clearly defined role, set out on Fat Dave's spreadsheet. Little Dave was to dig out the soil and flowers and fit the plastic liner, Fat Dave was to operate the wheel-barrow, while Big Dave had to deal with passers-by. But Big

Dave didn't need to deal with passers-by because no one in Pontefract paid any attention to the three Daves at all.

Come the night of the stag, each Dave sat on a stool next to his trough and began to drink through a long bendy straw. There were no other guests to cater for because the rest of the Shoreditch crowd had decided it would be more ironic not to come.

After an hour, the Daves began to feel cold sitting by their beer-filled troughs. It was quiet too. A few hardy smokers stood outside the nearby pubs looking into the middle distance, but apart from polite nods, they didn't call across to any of the Daves. No Dave rang or texted any of the other Daves because there was a strict no-mobile rule on stags, and the three Daves followed this to the letter because stags were about bonding and getting away from the world.

Are Friends Electric?

S HE LAID THE description cards on the coffee table and explained the different qualities of each friend. One was a good listener. One was up to date on the latest films. One made her laugh.

'There are certain people,' she slid two cards to one side, 'I still meet regularly. But the rest . . .' The remaining cards formed an untidy pile. 'I am severely behind with the rest. I just can't find the time. Phone calls, drinks, theatre trips, lunches. If I did all that was expected, I would have no days left in me.' At this point she began, as many do, to cry.

'It's like a big coat I have to live inside,' she whimpered, almost to herself.

Some people find these moments intrusive, but not he. He has had intensive training. 'Don't worry,' he said. 'We will select one of your favourites and transfer the qualities of your other friends to them. The others will simply,' he wiggled his fingers in the air, 'melt away.'

She looked at him with green eyes that swirled with wisps of grey. 'But the memories. I share many memories with some of these friends. Golden days.'

'Sometimes it feels as if the days are holding on to you,' he said, and reached across and touched her lightly on the arm. 'Shared memories can be simulated with ease. It's a very efficient service. I have many, many certificates. All over my walls.'

He noticed her little body quivering again and reached out and held her shoulders lightly in his hands. Her damp, perfumed warmth. 'All my certificates are in special frames. It's like a gallery. You must come and see them some time.'

She gulped, sucked in air and sobbed again. 'Your certificates?'

'Yes. Make an appointment with my secretary.'

'I will,' she said. 'When it's all over I will definitely do that.'

You Would Have

I WAS AT A fancy schmancy media party and I asked this girl what she did and she said she worked for the Gas Board.

'Oh yes,' I said, 'what do they do?' thinking the Gas Board was some Hoxton Square design agency.

She looked at me for a long time, then said, 'They deliver gas to people's homes. For heating and cooking.'

'Oh yes,' I said, 'I've heard of them.'

'You would have,' she said.

You would have. I thought that was very funny of her. I thought that was a very funny thing to say.

I Liked Everything

HERE WAS ANOTHER. In his nylon football shirt and glaring white trainers he stood in a numb trance in front of Landseer's Dignity and Impudence. A painting of cute animals. How predictable. The man was one of the hard-to-reach, a C2, D, and E. We were to embrace them, welcome them in. And if you thought C2, D and E was C3POs less cheeky brother, you'd be disappointed. Socio-economic groups, don't you know. Low income, low attainment, low, low, low. But not as low as you think. Dorothy, our Visitor Services Manager, told us with pride that C2, D and Es were not all from rough estates — oh, no. Many of the gallery's technicians and visitor staff were C2, D and E, so we shouldn't worry.

It was nice to know I was lower class. My preference of Salad Cream over mayonnaise provided a clue, but it was good to have it confirmed.

The man's eyes roamed all over Landseer's painting. He traced the brush marks with his fingers in the air. He looked away, then quickly back — to see if the eyes would follow him, perhaps? He stroked his chin as though something inside him was being slowly absorbed. Then he emitted a low moaning sound and, abruptly, tears began to flow.

What was the point? Allowing these people in was feeding strong meat to infants.

I went over. He looked at me with pale blue eyes that shone with tears.

'Our Landseer has made an impression.'

'Yes,' he said. 'I was standing in a gorgeous cathedral. Golden voices sang.'

This was preposterous. The man's responses were false, exaggerated for my benefit. Another fake. Had to be.

'You do realise,' I said, 'that this exhibition is limited to those community members who demonstrate deep, meaningful responses to the works of art. I'm sure, sir, that your responses to the art works are real, but I'm afraid you've been selected for a random test.'

We found a private room and I began my interrogation

'It wasn't just the Landseer,' he explained. 'I liked everything,' and he elaborated on his love of the visual arts, peppering his monologue with academic quotes off the internet.

We looked at each other across the desk. I knew and he knew I knew.

'What are we to do with you, Mr . . .?'

'Rainford.'

'Mr Rainford. You realise that faking a response to a publicly-funded work of art is a serious offence?'

His pale blue eyes unblinkingly held my gaze.

'Why pretend, Mr Rainford?'

He leaned back in his chair, his arms loose at his sides. 'The attribution in this exhibition is appalling. Take the so-called Manchester Madonna. And some of the Giottos . . .'

'Stop right there, mister. I am not here to defend this hang. Mr Rainford, you have been uncovered as a fraud and you know our policy very well. We are a public gallery and are responsible for ensuring that engagement between

members of the public and our works of art is meaningful.
We all remember what happened in Bury.'

Mr Rainford leaned forward and lowered his voice. 'My
dear,' he said. 'Many art works in galleries are forgeries. So
why should I not forge my response? Art is for forging. I not
only forge my responses, I forge art works too. Many works.
I have forged works of art which have elicited intense emotional responses. Which is the fake? The response, or the
art? Everything about art can be forged. In one city I forged
the interpretation panels. In another I forged the way-
marking signs. I forged the cakes in the gallery cafés. In
another city I replaced every doorknob with an identical
replica. No one guessed. In a town in West Cumbria I forged
a whole gallery. Only the art was real. I forged the money
used to pay artists. I forged artists too — trained people to
paint and sculpt, then sent them into galleries to run work-
shops. Then I moved on to the staff. How did we know the
gallery staff were real? Staff could be as easily forged as the
works of art for which they cared. After all, can you remember, Rosemary, when you began working at this Gallery?'

He knew my name. I tried to think back to a time before
I worked here, but Mr Rainford was right. Everything before
that point was hazy. It seemed I had always been here.

'It's true, Rosemary. You've been working for me. Now
you meet your creator.' He squeezed my cheek between
his thumb and forefinger. 'I made you well. You spotted me
right away as a faker. Found me out. You were meant to. My
work was of the highest standard, as ever. Well, well. The
forged art curator and forged aficionado. What will we do?'

I looked into his pale blue eyes. The eyes that had pretended to draw so such meaning from the paintings were
drawing things from me. Something relaxed inside me, as if
a tightened muscle I was previously unaware of had slack-

ened. I wasn't real. Nothing mattered. I reached across the table and touched Mr Rainford's hand.

'If it's all a game, then let's play,' I said. 'You and I will play well together.'

HALF HERE

Wooden Animals

THE WORD SET up home in my head. It attracted other similar words and eventually married one of them and had children. A community grew up in there, focussed around this word. No other word had a chance. The word was 'bespectacled', and it was planted by Mr Fisher when he found the speck of popcorn I'd missed in the foyer.

The foyer carpet was patterned with old-fashioned swirls and popcorn was hard for anyone to spot. What's more, the Hoover Mr Fisher supplied was not the best, but as he kept pointing out, times were hard in the last gasp world of independent cinemas. The Elland Rex, though performing well on family pictures, was still not grabbing the adults on weekday nights, and it didn't help if there was popcorn on the carpet.

He examined the speck of yellow on the tip of his finger and his jaw slackened with disgust. 'You know, Julie, I'm not being funny, but when was the last time you had your eyes tested?'

'I had them done the last time I had my head looked at,' I said, and he flew back into his office like he was on the end of an elastic band.

All of my family had good sight, not one of us wore glasses.

I had seven fans on Guardian Soulmates and two dates pencilled in, so I couldn't be bespectacled. The words it dragged in its wake — demure, retiring, librarian. It was true that when I watched a film nowadays, everything looked befogged, but I'd put this down to the Rex's dirty screen. Whenever there was a big expanse of white sky, the grease stains really stood out and Mr Fisher had even taken to asking distributors if particular films included many shots of bright sky, and if so, how long did they last?

At Elland opticians, I got no further than the window display; a row of giant spectacles perched on the wooden heads of moose, sheep, zebra and cows. How vulnerable these noble beasts looked in their glinting glasses, shifty even, and how sorry I felt for them, banished from their herds for becoming bespectacled.

That night it was a full house for Doubt, with Meryl Streep. For some reason they liked nun films in Elland. 'Everyone likes a nun film,' Mr Fisher said, as if it was common knowledge. 'Not like Nuns on the Run,' he added. 'Real nun films, like the Magdalene Sisters. The problem is, they never make enough.'

I watched Doubt, standing at the back, as usual, and noted how many of the nuns wore spectacles and how it changed their faces when they took them off. Glasses made you look weak. They made your eyes stand further out on your face. A predator creature has deep set, sharply-focussing eyes, and prey creatures big, blurry, protruding globes on the sides of their heads.

I thought of the wooden animals in the optician's window and looked at Meryl Streep in her glasses, worrying about whether Phillip Seymour-Hoffman was a paedophile, and thought of her dancing on the bed in Mamma Mia. I decided to make an appointment to see the contact lenses specialist.

Remaking the Moon

MASON'S HOUSE HAD no garden, no walls, no hedges, no borders of any kind, so the local historians who streamed past on their way to the fascinating sluice gates and flooded mine shaft stared through his window at him rudely as if he were a zoo exhibit. At first he glowered and shooed them away, but they never seemed perturbed. They would smile at Mason in that sarcastic way people with an interest in local history have, then saunter off, trailing their fingers along his brickwork. It was as if Mason and his house were public property, like a puppy or pregnant woman.

After many years of this, he decided to give the local historians something to stare at. Every Saturday he would set up a little tableaux; one day he would be playing a lute, another day dressed in Mexican wrestling regalia, grappling on the floor with a tailor's dummy. Today he was pretending to stuff a badger and there was sawdust and plastic eyes all over the place.

She was young for a local historian and from the way she tapped loudly on his window pane, it was possible she suspected Mason might be an automaton operated by the council's heritage curator. She had a mouth that looked as though it was smiling, even when it wasn't, and eyes that closed from time to time as if she were in some sort of ecstasy. Mason did something he had never done before.

He went to the front door and opened it.

She wore a green skirt with red tights, a yellow jumper and a purple hat. When Mason addressed her, she spoke to him in a breathless, hurried voice, closing her eyes in a weird half-asleep way.

'I'm from next door,' she said.

'Oh,' Mason said

'No one stops to look through my window any more. They all come straight to your place, to look at you.'

He paused for a moment to allow this information to settle.

'No one has paused at my window for a long, long time,' she added.

'I see,' Mason said. 'Maybe you should come in.'

Mason made some tea and chopped some fruit and they sat on the sofa together, eating and drinking slowly. When they had finished he took her hand in his and she let him, closing her eyes in that wistful way she had.

'Do you want to do a jigsaw?' Mason said.

'Yes,' she said.

Mason went to his puzzle cupboard, located the moon one and tipped the pieces on to the floor. Every piece looked exactly the same. They got down on their knees in the sawdust and plastic eyes and began to assemble it. Local historians looked in on them as they remade the moon. One of them, a round-faced bearded man, caught Mason's eye and winked and the man looked happier than any local historian Mason had ever seen, as if by watching Mason and the young woman remaking the moon, something had been added to him.

Do the Voice

I T BEGAN WITH the door to the balaclava cupboard. Its two-note see-saw creak, in descending thirds, sounded exactly like the uh huh catch phrase of the disturbed woman in Little Britain. I heard this every time I changed my balaclava, which was three times a week, and once I'd noticed it, my house became a polyphony of comedy quips. The moaning floorboard on the stair said Suit you, sir, and the bolts on the door went What a plonker, Rodney. Smothering the cacophony with ukelele practice didn't work, either. Underneath the tunes, I could still hear the wind rubbing a branch against the guttering, going What are the scores, George Dawes? and water curling through the radiator murmuring Don't tell them, Pike. The voices insinuated themselves into my sleep, to be born out into the day with me.

A jittery council man confirmed the infestation, but explained that eradication was expensive. Instead, he adjusted the noises to make them sound like songs.

These days, the Balaclava cupboard door plays 'Hey Jude', the low deep-stretched hum of the boiler is 'O Superman', and things are a little better. Sometimes, though, I must admit I miss the fridge clucking Stupid boy and the dish washer hissing You're my wife now. The phrases had a live, fleshy quality. Now a post-modern chill permeates everything. I'm even thinking of changing my balaclava for a Trilby.

Pathfinders

BEHIND THE BOARDS I get no light, but I don't miss the light and I don't miss Mam and Dad. I know they've got windows and light out there in soft-shit-town, but I prefer it here, where I've always been. I could rip the boards off, if I wanted —upstairs there's a whole window unsmashed— but it's safer to keep them up. The bulldozers will come soon, anyway; the pathfinders were crawling around again yesterday. I kept my head low.

On a Saturday I go to Barking Mad and watch the woman blow-drying the poodles. One day I said, 'Would you give me a wash, missus?' I was looking at the hot soapy water and I was freezing cold and I really thought it would be so lovely. 'You could dry me on the table like the poodle,' but she threw me a filthy look and said I was a pervy little bastard, and I hadn't thought of it like that, but when I did I got a semi, I admit.

Along the edge of the estate stretch long, black hoardings with Pathfinder logos all over. You could run away from those hoardings. They want you to run away from them.

Abby said she'd meet me at the table and chairs. The table and chairs was a civilised place to meet. It was covered by a corrugated plastic roof, so we could meet there even in the rain. Abby had brought a condom and I had too, so we thought it would be romantic if I wore both, so I did — super-sexy, super-safe.

No one goes to the table and chairs now. It was for smokers from the pub, but the pub's all shuttered-up, like everything else. I like to go there with Abby. It's like being in a real house, but on a stage so everyone can see in. One night I said let's break in to Barking Mad and we did and she put me in the big dog bath. It smelt a bit, dog hairs all over, but there was loads of hot water and we both got in. We laughed and laughed and splashed about, and then I sat on the drying table and she picked up the big dryer the lady uses on the poodles and blew hot hair all over me and it was gorgeous; I was the happiest I'd felt for months. I wondered if I should dress up in one of the little dog coats they sold and crawl about on all fours, maybe even bark, and then they'd leave me alone, let me carry on living boarded-up.

I don't have to stay, there are ways out — motorways, canal-ways, railways — but I don't want a way out. All I'm looking for is a way to stay. A sign behind the table and chairs says DANGER — DEEP EXCAVATIONS. Why don't people make tunnels any more? Secret tunnels people could live in when their mum and dad run out of medicine.

Emergency Kisses

NO ONE DROPS in to enquire about industrial breathing equipment on Saturdays, so when I spotted her on the CCTV, I was surprised and had to run out from the back where I'd been watching Football Focus. I pulled up my tie and fastened my jacket so that I wasn't scruffy. She was carrying a guitar and I asked if she'd come to give me a song, but she didn't laugh. She said the guitar was cheap in Save The Children and it was for her husband who she was hoping would learn to sing.

I watched her while she wandered about in reception looking at the photo of the man in the cellophane body suit and the glass cases with the pumps and the filters, then after a time she came over to the desk. She said that she'd dropped in because she thought we might be able to help her husband. His breathing was irritating, especially when she was trying to watch telly. It was worse during the quiet bits in films, and horrible when he was looking at the horses in the paper. She imitated the sounds he made and looked at me, but I didn't say anything because you don't interfere, do you? If it wasn't his breathing, it was something else. He would ask about the programme she was watching like, who is that man and why is he going through the woman's drawers, and she'd say, watch it properly if you're interested, but he would sit with the horse paper and watch

54

sneakily from the side, never with his full face towards the screen. He was only interested in bits. The doctor said he should learn the clarinet, as this was good for breathing control, and when she said they couldn't afford one, the doctor suggested singing, and that's why she'd got the guitar because he liked Eric Clapton and maybe this would inspire him.

She asked if there was something we sold that she could clamp to his face to make his breathing quieter, like a silencer device. I explained that everything we stocked was for industrial and emergency purposes, but she didn't seem put off and asked if I would demonstrate how to fit a gas mask using the mannequin we have behind reception, so I said she could come round this side — this was a Saturday, remember — and I showed how the tubes go into the mouth and how it locks. I've seen the sales guy demonstrate it loads of times. She was fascinated, so I got her a chair and told her everything I knew about breathing equipment. When she heard I was a guitarist she asked me to play, and I did 'Take It Easy' by The Eagles. It was her who spotted the hospitality wine in the back and then everything seemed to get out of hand.

Celia's Mum's Rat

I WAS ALONE, AWAY from home, and bored, so I lay on the hotel bed and scrolled through the names in my mobile phone. It was then I came across the strange entry: Celia's mum's rat.

I had no idea Celia's mother owned a rat. And if Celia's mother owned a rat, why had she felt the need to buy it a mobile phone? And why had I, at some point, needed the rat's number, and needed it frequently enough to enter it into the phone's memory? Or, rather, felt the need to know that if the rat called, I would know who it was. Maybe I had decided to avoid the rat's calls, or at least wanted time to prepare an excuse as to why I wouldn't be able to assist the rat? Yet, surely if Celia's mum's rat was important enough to own its own phone, it would have a name? After all, we didn't call Celia's mum's boyfriend 'Celia's mum's boyfriend'. We called him Raymond.

I imagined the sleek, smug-faced rodent lying on a miniature chaise longue, the mobile clamped to its ear, squeaking away to other rats with similar luxurious accessories. Budgies have mirrors, hamster have wheels, what do rats have? Phones. Was there a computerised system to translate the rat's squeaks into rudimentary requests? Like food, bedding, water? Handling, maybe?

I looked about me at the bleak hotel room. The clock said

11:30. Celia's mum's rat might feel a sudden desire to be handled at any time. Celia's mum and Raymond might be out. My phone would ring and the robot voice would say: I WANT YOU TO HANDLE ME NOW, PLEASE.

It was a chilling thought. I turned off my phone and tried to sleep, but the idea of the rat was adhesive. The phone would ring, the demand would be made, and I would drop everything. To assist Celia's mum's rat was my purpose in life.

HALF GONE

We Are the Real Time Experiment

I DRIVE IT BECAUSE it's classic. Nothing to do with Trotter and Company. Basically, it's an enclosed motorbike with the same qualities of lightness and freedom. It even leans over on bends, and on a gusty motorway its plastic body is like a sail. Can you imagine being lifted off the ground at seventy miles an hour? That's an adrenaline sport. That's the screaming edge.

Arthur doesn't agree. He says that it's unseemly for an older man, especially when the older man wears a hat. Arthur says there's no such thing as old people. Old people have been eradicated. No generations. Just people living together in a perpetual present. He also hates the collection of tin toys I lug to and from boot sales in the back of the plastic rocket. He says I only like pretty things made of tin, not practical things, that I have a penchant for the cute, and that is not a good trait for an older man.

So when I went to the post office to check whether they had stuck up my card: WANTED: TIN TOYS, PEDAL CARS, POP GUNS, ETC, I knew right away who had handwritten the extra line at the bottom: OLD VERMIN TRAPS, in an untidy scrawl, and I confronted him with it as soon as I got home.

'Tin vermin traps are a classic 1930's design,' he said. 'Every bit as collectable as tin cars. Hunter Davies has kept every tax disc he's ever owned and probably every toenail clipping as well. Keep everything or nothing, I say. We are the real-time experiment.'

Arthur recently de-cluttered and now owned nothing but a pension book, a skateboard and a Led Zeppelin boxed-set.

'Your life.' he said. 'Written, directed and produced by you, but as yet unedited.'

'Tin toys remind us of better, simpler times.' I said. 'No one wants to remember breaking a rat's spine with a steel spring.'

'Maybe those are exactly the things we should remember,' he said. 'I'm going down the skate park because I'm not a drooling crumbly who lives in an Oxfam shop and drives about in a doll's shoe.'

After he'd gone, I set off to the post office to replace the defaced card. I didn't want people ringing me up and talking about dead rats. Collecting is not about memories, it's about forcing something out of the past and into the future, bringing it into the light. I took Arthur's dry cleaning with me to drop off on the way. He likes his suits just so; he wouldn't allow the trousers to go through the washing machine, whatever the instructions say. 'My body might be immortal,' he always says, 'but my image isn't.'

Delivered by Sharks

M RS HARRISON MADE the sign herself: ALL TROU-
SERS ONE POUND. But she didn't expect Mrs Pugh
to follow it to the letter. Leather trousers were a high-value
item. She knew who Mrs Pugh had sold them to as well:
Bill Smethwick. She saw him wearing them at the Town
Hall hairdressers. They were too tight and when he moved
about with that over-chiropracted slink he had, they made
a whistling sound. Bill Smethwick was Mrs Pugh's latest
crush. He ran the online war memorial and Mrs Pugh loved
the idea of him sitting up late, pressing the little levers that
operate the internet.

It didn't surprise Mrs Harrison that Bill Smethwick
bought the leather trousers. He was totally down with youth
culture. The last time he was in the shop he'd talked about
the kind of ceremony he'd have if he got married again. The
mix CD for the limo would be totally 2-step garage. 2-step
garage was a new art form, he explained, guitar music
hadn't moved on. He would have a giant water tank in the
church so that the ring could be delivered by a baby shark.
He liked saying those words: mix CD, 2-step garage, baby
shark, and would look at you like he was challenging you to
ask him, what's a mix CD? How can a baby shark deliver a
ring? But Mrs Harrison never gave him the pleasure.

She was due at the shop for her shift soon and would

overlap with Mrs Pugh by half an hour. Overlap time was important, the area manager said. Mrs Pugh would be watching the window, hoping for Bill Smethwick to pop in on his way to the Town Hall hairdressers, where he also liked to tell the ladies about the mix CD and the baby shark and no doubt boast about the leather trousers he got for a pound from the ladies who were too old and stupid to know the value of anything.

Previously Loved

ONE MINUTE I was on the landing, the next in a floating, luminous space, pulsing with blinding light, with no centre, no edges, no up nor down. Dozens of men were sitting on white sofas, staring ahead, and I joined them. The rapturous humming of a thousand angels filled the air. White robes hung loosely about me and soft moccasins were on my feet. Everyone looked the same; we were in a cheap science fiction series. I asked one of the men what I was doing there and he smiled slowly, as if recognising a lost relative, and asked me in an awed half-whisper what I remembered last. I told him I had gone upstairs and couldn't remember why, and had stood on the landing trying to recall. Suddenly, I was here.

It had been the same for them all. Gone upstairs, tried to remember why, and couldn't.

'Had there had been a mighty flash?' he said

I nodded.

'If you can remember why you went upstairs, you will return.'

I asked if anyone had ever managed to get back to the real world, but he couldn't remember.

'We are not very reliable on recent history,' he said.

I sat and thought. Rusty cogs ground in my head, but nothing came. My mind seemed empty of all facts. If asked,

I would have been unable to explain even the concept of upstairs, or the idea of a house, or describe my town, my wife, or what I did during my days on earth.

After a time, a salesman asked if I was interested in buying the sofa I was occupying; if not that one, maybe a small corner set—currently on special offer and available in leather as well as linen. I could plump for brand new or previously loved.

I signed a buy-now-pay-later deal for a new one, at a very reasonable interest rate. I wasn't stupid. Owning your sofa is the sensible choice if you spend long periods sitting on it. Renting is dead money. After all, the sofa might grow in value, while all you have to do is sit and think and stare.

The Ones we Left

IT WAS DONALD'S first time as winchman. He looked out over the lip of the helicopter. Who would have thought the canals held so much? Tongues of filthy, brown gunge lapped over bungalow roofs; the roofs that hadn't been sliced off like the tops of boiled eggs and sent spinning into trees where they now hung, pierced by branches. The typhoon had ripped off walls too, allowing Donald a dolls-house view of intimate interiors — coats draped over chairs, abandoned shoes, expectant sofas. Gaping human shapes, yearning to be filled.

The helicopter descended into the hotel quarter. Pale smudges in exposed bedrooms resolved into heads, the grey heads of dozens of sleeping couples. Lover's town, said the brochures, and with that in mind, they came. Recapturing an essence. Then, one afternoon, it's back to the hotel for a snooze and everything stops. Frozen.

In identical positions they lay, folded together like spoons, the man's arms about the woman, leg draped over protectively, as if he'd known. They slept on, oblivious, innocent, happy. Donald wondered what thoughts they'd had as they snoozed, unaware of a hundred other couples lying in the same positions, holding each other in the same way. He wondered how they had arrived at this point in their lives, with this particular partner, in this particular town, at this particular time. Were they interchangeable? If he swapped the partners round, would they notice? Another grumbling husband or disenchanted wife, each enjoying and detesting more or less the same things as the last?

He climbed into the strop and attached a hammer to the Grabbit hook. Down, down, down they went, as low as was safe, until they were hovering above a roofless hotel, the blades ruffling the surface of the newly-formed lake. Beneath the wop wop wop of the helicopter blades, he heard music sailing up—Sinatra, 'Under My Skin'. The pilot retracted the cable and drew him out of the aircraft into a position hanging just outside the door. The cloud from the chemical works had dispersed, but he still needed the mask. As he was lowered, Donald kept his arms tightly at his sides, avoiding the temptation to grasp the cable and throw himself out of the strop as he'd done in training. As he descended in this position through the shattered hotel roof, he felt ridiculous, like an Irish dancer.

The sleeping old couple were strewn with storm litter—leaves, plastic bags, supermarket flyers. It was as the doctors had said: coma, caused by the chemical explosion. Donald began to clear away the debris, because a polythene bag sucked into the engine intake could be disastrous. Then he fastened the couple into stretchers. He secured the karabiners and sent the woman up. She hung limply, arms and legs thrown out in a star-jump, swivelling on the pivot as she ascended through the downdraught. If her husband woke, he would assume she was on her way to heaven.

Winch them up and get them to hospital where they'd be monitored till they came round. That was his job. But could they save them all? What about the ones they would inevitably leave behind? So many old couples, snoozing happily in the town for lovers, their arms about each other, their favourite music playing. Who was he to spoil it?

Shaky Ron Versus the Chewing Gum Robots

A PACK OF COCKNEY stag-night wankers woke me up by chucking kebab sauce over my blanket. That's when I first saw the little things. Hundreds of them, like wee shiny beetles, skittering along the pavement, their little metal legs tip-tapping on the floor, their pointy teeth gnashing away at the gum. My first thought was that it was the mega-lager goggles, cos you often see crawly things when you've taken on a pile. But it was real. I know. I watched them every night. Every night as they streamed out from under their lamppost and went to work getting rid of the gum. Only the acid from their slender nozzle noses remained, fizzing on the pavement.

Training them wasn't easy, but the next pissed-up dickhead who messed with me got a surprise. That night, while he was sleeping, my wee metallic chums climbed out of his pocket and in the morning he found that his face had gone.

HALF AWAKE

Double Digging

GLORIA'S FACE WAS on the banknotes in nice town. Her smile throbbed with evil E numbers. She was never horrible, never mean, and never made a juicy dig at the girls in promotions. But today, dental anaesthetic had tugged the corners of her mouth into an exaggerated sad-clown face and, for the first time in Gloria's life, she looked like mortal sin.

Benjamin didn't normally register Gloria's presence, but when he caught sight of her sour, crushed expression, he stopped her and told her that suddenly he felt a connection. She had a dark, adhesive quality that beckoned. He scanned his desk and his eyes landed on a fern growing in a yogurt pot, which he picked up and handed to her.

'Come to my allotment on Sunday,' he said.

Gloria took the fern over to her desk. Everyone smiled and offered words to ease her lonely desperation. Her inbox for the first time contained the Drinky Poos Email. She looked from the email to the fern, and silver voices sang in her head.

On Sunday, she watched Benjamin dribble seeds from his curled palm into holes he'd jabbed into the chocolaty soil with his big fingers. He smiled at her, she scowled back though numb cheeks, and he laughed.

The dentist could offer her daily injections for a limited

period only. It was strictly unethical. But what would she tell Benjamin and the others when her smile returned? How could she go back to happy when miserable was so much fun?

Away Day

IMAGINE YOU ARE happy. Picture it. You, happy. It can be you, yes. You can be happy, like everyone else. Picture it now. You, a happy person, doing happy things, without a care in the world. Have you got it? Can you see yourself? What are you doing? Don't tell me, I know. You are in the countryside. You are with friends and family, the people you love. It's a sunny day. You are sharing food and drink—wine, even. You are drinking from a paper cup, a tablecloth is laid on the grass.

It is a picnic. You are having a picnic.

Everybody's idea of happiness involves a picnic. A picnic has everything a human being needs. If there were more picnics, the world would be a happier place. And what do our clients want from us but happiness? Isn't that why they come here? Why the health service contracts us to deliver the service?

Next month the clinical psychology team are going on a picnic. Details are attached, along with a map. Please wear appropriate shoes and clothing.

Gelling

BARRY KNOWS WHAT they are thinking. They are thinking he looks like a toaster with a clock on the side. What if he shot them all? Took out a gun and said, 'This will help you gel, this will help you bond.'

He goes outside to the car. Stands for a moment listening to the birds twittering. Do birds know what's going to happen next? He opens the boot and takes out two boxes. The larger box is long, coffin-shaped, and from inside comes the sound of scrabbling and faint peeping. The smaller box emits no sound and has the word 'Dylan' written on the side. A door on the front, like a cat flap. Like one of those boxes pigeon racers use. Clocks on the top too, but with clear utility.

The trainees watch as Barry places the coffin-shaped box in the centre of the table and the smaller one next to him at the head.

Don't make fun of them, Barry.

The scratching noise comes from the big box again and everyone looks at it. The sound comes in waves, then stops as if whatever is inside is resting.

Barry smiles. The trainees will think his teeth are over-flossed. You can over-floss. You can overdo everything. Barry knows this. That's why he is a consultant.

'What's in the boxes?'

The speaker has a too-much-dope-wide-frog-smile-small-independent-hardware-store face.

Barry looks at the names he has written on his pad in the shape of how people are sitting. 'Andy, is it? Yes, Andy, the boxes are important.'

Barry is a toaster with a clock on the side.

It is disparate. A tourist information centre, a gallery, a literature agency, a restaurant, a couple of design companies, some front of house staff, some building managers, a caretakers, some cleaners, and a technician.

Barry removes Margaret's lid. Margaret is his favourite marker. She has been lucky and he doesn't know what he would do if she dried up. So he never writes with her, just flips off her cap and grips her in his fingers, using an inferior pen to make his marks.

One for playing, one for keeps.

'Imagine Industry House as a village. The passages, corridors and meeting rooms are village lanes and the window ledges flowerbeds. How can we breath life into these public spaces?'

They will know if you hate them. Don't hate them.

The big box emits the scrabbling sound again and, as if ringing in sympathy, a thin, unhappy whining comes from whatever is trapped inside the smaller box.

'Cricket in the corridor;' says one.

'Giant pie making.'

'Burn effigies of local councillors,' says another

'Morris dancing,' says one.

'Incest,' says another.

Barry springs to the flip chart and scribbles with the inferior marker pen. He doesn't write 'consultant goes on killing rampage'. He writes down what they say about the village he has put them in. He doesn't write 'if she didn't love me then why did she come to the video installation at the cathedral?'

He has locked them in a village of his invention. He will feast them, impale them, then torch the fools.

Remember you are not a god.

He bounces up and down while he writes, his shoulders quivering, his legs vibrating.

Show them energy and they will take it. They will absorb it.

They say things and he makes bullets. His face is wide open, his eyes expanded, his eyebrows in his hair. He has not had an electric shock. He looks friendly. Market researchers will stop him in the street, a prime example of a certain segment.

But no one looks at Barry or his flip chart. They look at the two boxes that make noises. They read the word 'Dylan' on the side of the smaller one and wonder what it means. The big box trembles with the vibrations from whatever is inside and the little box bounces on the table as its inhabitant thumps madly at the sides.

Barry moves the trainees on to the next stage. This will be the best stage. Barry will develop ideas of hubs, of water-cooler places, of points where ways intersect. Industry House will be an oasis of warmth and conviviality. Industry House will be a building where the default is stop and chat. When staff in Industry House speak they will be above the line.

He draws the line on the flip chart.

'What words might be above the line?'

They don't know.

'How about: "that's fantastic, Fiona, that's tremendous, Fiona, that's amazing Fiona. I would be delighted to do that for you, Fiona." When we speak above the line, we think above the line and when we think above the line we become above the line and then above the line things happen.'

'Who's Fiona?' one says, softly.

Barry has been waiting for this one. He has shown himself. The muted, sincere one; a storm of abuse is vaulted in those whispers.

Barry consulted his diagram of names. 'Michael, isn't it? You are wondering who Fiona is. Fiona is a construct for today's course. She is all of you. You are no longer individuals. You are Fiona.'

If he makes the trainees into Fiona and they learn to love him, then Fiona will love him.

Don't make people pretend to be Fiona.

I won't.

I will, though.

Don't purse your lips.

Michael told Barry in his soft voice that he didn't want to be Fiona. He wanted to be Michael.

He would give Michael the job of opening the door and letting Dylan out.

Don't purse your lips. Pursing his lips means they will know that if he attended their niece's 18th birthday party, he would spit in the hummus.

He didn't spit, he dipped a cracker after he'd taken a bite, it wasn't the same as spitting in the hummus.

It was the same. It was his spit in the hummus. He may as well have hawked up a frothy green one, lobbed it into the centre and stirred it with his dick.

Barry thought back to his research. The Industry House caretaker was called Roy and he lived in a narrow boat and kept a tarantula in his window to ward off burglars.

Never let them know which bridge you're moored under.

Roy told Barry about the old Industry House. There were

lots of different organisations then, too: the Archaeology Unit, the Open College, the People's Trust, the Community Gallery, the writers forum, the digital development people, the Chamber of Commerce, the Dept of Continuing Education. The people of these organisations never spoke to each other. Each business was resolutely independent, insulated empires where strange breeds evolved with quirky characteristics peculiar to that place and that place alone.

They held separate Christmas parties.

But Barry needed the hubs, the water-cooler moments, the pivots, the forums.

The tarantula in the boat window shuffled behind its glass.

'Did anything, anything at all, ever bring them together?'

'There was a corn warehouse near the river. They pulled it down and the rats that lived there had nowhere to go, so they came to Industry House. A man was hired, it was his job. He was a rat catcher. He had a small terrier dog called Dylan and this dog could shake a dozen rats to death in an afternoon. Everyone stood in the garden and watched. They spoke to each other about how awful it was, and how horrible the rats were, and how it was gruesome yet fascinating to see Dylan at work, doing his natural thing.'

To author an event, a bonding session. To make things gel. Minds are corridors, staircases, foyers, atriums. Open it all up, make the spaces real. The trainees are Fiona and will forgive him for the hummus and come with him to the cathedral for the art installation.

He indicates that Michael should approach the box with Dylan on the side. Andy is holding the catch on the big box.

Soon everyone will be together.

Candy Girl

H E P U R S E D H I S lips over the Winnie the Pooh mug and released a glop of frothy saliva before turning to find me watching from the doorway.

'For Farrah,' he explained, wiping his mouth with the back of his hand. 'Team Leader Farrah, Bitch from Space Farrar. My downtime is well fucked-up.'

Sugar after sugar went in on top as he sang softly, 'Farrah, you might be sweet enough as it, but here we go — one, two, three,' stirring hard, round and round.

After he'd gone, I dropped a teabag into Jayne's Everton mug and filled it from the urn, thinking how the cow would be analysing my quarterlies right now. I squeezed the teabag with the spoon, staining the water pale brown. A sign above the urn said that there were no kitchen fairies.

One Thing Deeply

I CAN'T REMEMBER THE last time I deliberately made a colleague cry, in fact I don't believe I ever have or would, but Nathan, our new guru, took this as hard evidence I was too nice, and vowed that he and I working together would unleash the nasty in me, whatever it took. It would be a challenge, especially when he discovered that even after picturing the fat, loud head-of-marketing twunt, or one of the twitchy, scuttling research wonks, or a human resource tick-boxer, or a cartoon-socked IT tech, I couldn't think of anything sarcastic or unpleasant to say.

'What do you picture inside yourself, Dave?'

I am a catholic, and inside me floats a wisp of white mist — my soul. Each time I commit a wrong deed, a black mark appears; fully wipeable for venial sins, but in the case of mortal sin, removable only by catholic confession. I explained this to Nathan.

'Good, good, Dave. I like that. What's in the middle of this clump of mist?'

I focussed hard and saw a grey panel with a red switch in its centre.

'Good, very good. That's the nasty. That's your nasty. Together we will switch that nasty on.'

We sat together and concentrated, eyes tightly shut, and

slowly, inside the clump of mist, a hand came into view and, on Jonathan's command, flipped the switch.

There was a long, dying gasp and something heavy plummeted down a deep shaft.

'I want to hear about people storming out of rooms, screaming, hitting you and smashing things.' Jonathan said. 'After that, we will move onto dealing with your time management issues.'

But despite flipping on the nasty switch, it wasn't easy. I told Heather in communications that Cliff Richard was dead, but she told me not to be a twat; I told Ray McCarthy he had Britpop hair; I asked Grianne if she knew she looked like fat comic Jo Brand, but all they did was smile; understanding, pitying. What was wrong? Evil should be pumping out like black milk.

I gave up and sat next to Ben who was struggling with his script for the hundred-best-motorcycle-and-side-car comedy moments, a programme inspired by a scene in 'The Office' when Gareth climbs into a sidecar belonging to a swinging couple. Comedy motorcycle and side-car moments like this had not occurred as often in the history of television and film as our producer expected, and Ben was struggling for the other ninety-nine clips. The scenes he had found were obscure: Jerry Lewis, Laurel and Hardy, a seventies sitcom called Lucky Fellah (a bubble car, not a motorbike and sidecar), On The Buses, and several war films. Ben was watching a scene from Wallace and Gromit when I told him my feelings about sidecars. A sidecar upsets the balance of a motorbike, destroying its grace as it tilts round a bend, dragging it back when it vrooms away from a junction, sucking out its sex, its danger, its dark, seductive beauty. Attaching a sidecar to a bike was like bolting a lead coffin to a butterfly.

Ben didn't look at me or say anything. I could hear him breathing, very deeply, very slowly. He was looking at a frozen image from Wallace and Gromit, and mouthing to himself the text that ran above it: 'the top one-hundred motorcycle and sidecar comedy moments: number seven.' Abruptly, he pushed the computer's off switch—without saving, closing, or logging off—and picked up his bag. While buttoning his coat, he looked at me in an intense way I'd never seen before, as if he could see a universe in my face, a world of opportunities, almost lost but still within reach.

After Ben left, I went round the whole office giving everyone else my views on his or her project, and each of them did the same thing. Soon the office was empty but for me. I looked out of the window to the street below at the line of staff streaming out of the front door.

I returned to Nathan's office, but he'd also gone, and I sat alone in the consulting room staring at his filing cabinet. I lifted down one of his management text books—Discover Your Emotional Animal—and turned a few pages. I was a hedgehog. A fox knows many things; a hedgehog knows one thing deeply. The book recommended I should keep a picture of my emotional animal on my wall for inspiration, so I ripped out the picture of the hedgehog and took it over to my workstation.

Before that day, the personalisation of desks was prohibited.

Don't Thank Me, Thank the Moon's Gravitational Pull

CHRISTINE WAS MANAGING the office relocation, an opportunity to take her mind off the break-up with Malcolm. Malcolm, however, was Health and Safety, and everything had to be approved by him.

She indicated with a polished fingernail the position of the new building, but Malcolm moaned, shook his head and did nervy jazz hands.

'You've forgotten something vital. The building's relationship to where most of our staff live.'

Christine explained about public transport.

'I was wondering whether it's east or west. I only ever work west of where I live, so that on the way to and from work, the sun is never in my eyes.'

'But you come to work on the tube.'

'I have a strong sense of the planet. Even underground I know where I am in relation to the sun.'

She agreed to go with him to a cellar bar so he could demonstrate this skill, and it did explain something. The time he'd consulted a compass before making love, claim-

ing the moon's gravitational pull enhanced his performance, he'd been lying.

HALF ALONE

How the Taste Gets In

B ARRY'S DAD DIDN'T have long left, so Barry tried to get him whatever he asked for and you never know, maybe Ewan McCall, poet of canal and factory, did play the Longfield Suite in Prestwich, and if he did, maybe he did stick a plectrum behind the mirror in the dressing room.

The doors to the Longfield Suite concert room were clothed with heavy curtains and Barry parted them to reveal a row of wheeled hospital beds on which lay a group of middle-aged ladies dressed in chiffon, bells, and feathers.

Belly dancers.

But the ladies weren't belly dancing. Tubes in their arms led to plastic bags filled with dark liquid. He wondered whether this was some secret government experiment, but an examination of the posters in the foyer revealed that a woman called Felicity ran a belly dance session every Saturday morning. The blood donor session followed it and the ladies must have agreed to help out.

But who would want belly dancer's blood? A real belly dancer's, possibly, but these women? Middle-class council workers with a meaningless hunger for the exotic. His father required a blood transfusion every month, and Barry knew what he would say if he discovered the blood was from a Prestwich belly dancer.

A couple of nurses were laughing with Felicity, the

chocolate-haired dancing instructor, who was demonstrating some moves. Behind a screen sat a large blue box with red tape handles.

That night he sat with his feet up on the box of belly dancer's blood watching *Top Gear* back-to-back on Dave and drinking lager. The box wouldn't fit in the fridge so he didn't know what do with it.

In an advert break he picked up his lager and went to the window. He looked out at the tomato plants his father had insisted he put in. The brand was Outdoor Girl, so everything fitted, and he took a sachet of belly dancer's blood outside and dribbled it slowly onto the soil.

A couple of months of this treatment gave him the best crop of tomatoes he'd every seen, and when he took one to his father, the old man sliced it in two, lifted it to his nose and inhaled, long and deep.

'That, my son, is a tomato,' he said. 'I want to know everything you did to get it like that. Sit down and tell me,'

Barry sat and spoke to his father for a long time, longer than he'd ever spoken to him over one single period in his life. The fact that it might have been shreds of Ewan McCall's plectrum sprinkled into the feed made his father laugh, and it was nice, because he didn't used to laugh much, at least not when family members were around.

Desire Lines

GEOFFREY DISCOVERED THEM in a shallow pool in the middle of the site, corkscrewing madly, flashing tell-tale-orange spotted bellies and purple frilled combs. Clumps of grey jelly floated at the edge of the pond, pulsing with black pinpricks of new life.

Great crested newts.

The Poppyfield project was dead when the Environment Agency found out. The spawn would have to be allowed to hatch and the newts moved to a safe place, taking the project into autumn and beyond and then waiting, waiting, waiting.

Hopelessness pounced. This moonscape was supposed to become a gorgeous enclosure of air and light, fizzing with footsteps, laughter and dreams. It was to be a building that would reach up and touch the hand of god. Now, all those dreams would be lost. Millions of pounds, too. But that wasn't the point. The point was Geoffrey's father, who was invited to the topping off, possibly the only opportunity for him to see one of Geoffrey's buildings.

Something inside Geoffrey swelled as he imagined his father reading Geoffrey Lange, Lead Architect etched on a plaque. That's if he would even understand who Geoffrey was; the progress of his disease was horrifying, whole sections of his personality had been eaten away, like there was some evil Pacman bleeping through his head, munching cell after cell after cell.

Since his father went into the hospice, Geoffrey had experienced an urgent desire to create. There hadn't been a lot for his father to be proud of till now. Geoffrey had ditched university, there was the drugs, then the gambling, then the depression, then the affair. Then Sharon and the kids had left, and who could blame them? But now he was putting things right. The Poppyfields development would put things right. He had a new love, Althea, he was in contact with the kids, and he'd picked up his architecture where he'd left off and graduated with a First. If anything, his period of dissolution had nourished his new, successful self, offering a fresh angle on everything. Buildings require spontaneity, spaces where things no one had thought of could happen, spaces for paths others would make, so-called desire lines, imaginary gossamer threads that marked the routes real people would eventually tread. The architect's job was to make these desire lines real.

Normally, when you found newts, you rang the newt wrangler—yes, there is such a thing, Geoffrey knew him—a pleasant round-spectacled fellah called Norman who supported Carlisle United. But Geoffrey couldn't ring Norman. What he did instead was drive to B & Q, where he bought fishing nets, buckets, gloves and a giant tub of fish food.

It was hard work, rounding up the newts. They wriggled and slithered, they really didn't want to leave their pond. But if just one of these rare creatures was discovered, work would stop. He'd seen it with bats, voles and certain uncommon flowers. With some species he could understand the concern. But he had no idea why it was so important to preserve these ugly, slimy little beasts that crawled about unseen by anyone most of the time.

He tossed the last few newts into his bucket and shovelled the spawn in on top. But where to take them? He couldn't take them home because Althea hated anything creepy-crawly. Neither could he take them to another pond because Norman the newt wrangler had told him newts would travel miles back to the ponds where they were born.

So he took them to his father's house, which had lain empty since his he went into care.

The bath tap belched out gobbets of rust and he waited until a clear stream flowed, then inserted the plug and tipped the creatures in. But the newts didn't seem to like this sterile tub. They darted franticly about, their feet slithering against the porcelain. They would be missing their lovely bubbling, burping, pond. Also, he thought, weren't newts amphibians? Couldn't they drown? To be on the safe side, and to make it all the more homely, he gathered soil, stones and branches from the garden and spread this debris over the floor. Then he blocked off the overflow and filled the bath up to the rim so they could climb out.

He watched them for a time as flakes of food brought them gulping and gobbling to the surface. One of them seemed to make eye contact and Geoffrey touched its nose with his fingertip and sighed deeply.

Geoffrey was watching the first foundation post go in when he got the call. His father had gone walkabout. The last time his father did this he was found in Woolworth's in his dressing gown; the time before, asleep in a phone box, naked. But this time was different. The care assistant said that he'd been seen entering his old house. He still had keys, and he'd walked the five miles in his slippers. She wondered if Geoffrey could fetch him back. The old man was confused and anything could happen.

He got to his father's house to find that many newts had escaped and were crawling all over the property. His father was upstairs in the bathroom, sitting on the toilet in his tartan dressing gown and shiny slippers, holding a newt on his lap and stroking it as though it were a kitten. Geoffrey sat down on the floor next to him among the soil, stones, branches and squirming newts, and took his father's skinny, liver-spotted hand in his.

His father had tears in his eyes.

'They want me to look after them,' his father said. 'No one cares about them.'

Geoffrey looked at his father's thin, bare ankles.

'They're OK, Dad. People are working hard to protect them.'

'They don't feel at home in here. Anyone can see that.'

The sky grew dark and his father fell asleep. Geoffrey imagined the newts leaving the house through the front door and marching in columns down the road towards the pond.

Geoffrey's beautiful building would never be finished.

To Cause Amusement

I WATCHED THE HORRIFIED faces of the funeral guests as the box with Roland inside floated off and I couldn't understand why they were so upset. It is necessary to carry out the wishes of the dead, even if those wishes have never been expressed. At least, that was my view.

'I want the Oyster Cult blasting out in the church,' was all Roland had said. But the Oyster Cult spoke volumes.

Seeing the two shops side by side inspired me, and I remembered putting my hands out to form a balance and saying to the man, 'Funeral parlour, party balloons, funeral parlour, party balloons. I don't know. It's just — it makes you think.'

The funeral director smiled at me slowly, as you would at a troubled and much-discussed child. 'I can see that the deceased was well-loved. It's very difficult, I know. But don't worry, Mr Jenkins. The company will take it from here.'

It had sounded like a script.

'Is that a script?' I had said. 'I'm not being critical. I just wondered if it was standard phrases you learn to say. I'm interested in people's jobs.'

The funeral director went back inside and I stood for a time looking from the memorial wreathes in one window to the garish inflatables in the other. Then I went inside.

'Do you sell balloons in sad colours?'

'If you think yellow and red are sad.'

'I do, actually,' I said. 'But no one else does. That's my problem.'

'We can order anything you like, sir.'

Under its canopy of black helium balloons, Roland's coffin rose higher and higher till it was over the M62, the highest motorway in England. Up, up and up the box went, over Saddleworth and off into the distance; a grey smudge under a cloud of black, ascending into Roland's heavy metal heaven.

Spoilt Victorian Child

I SAW THE AD on the internet and thought, what the hell? I had no kids of my own, probably wouldn't have time, so why not go for it?

I didn't realise the child was Victorian at first. I thought it was just grumpy. But when it asked for a sing-song around the piano instead of plugging in the Xbox, I knew that I'd been done. The knickerbockers should have been a clue.

I'd read an article about the trend for adopting Victorian children. They were cheap to maintain as they ate little, had no desire for expensive trainers and were unable to use mobile phones. Yet I hadn't seen many around these parts. Until now.

But still, it was a child, so I made the best of it. I tried every possible distraction the twenty-first century had to offer, but nothing worked. The child was continually bored.

That was, until it found the flyer for the Art Treasures of the UK exhibition. As soon as it read about the paintings and artefacts to be displayed in Manchester Art Gallery, it became agitated with joy. I was to take it to the exhibition without delay—without delay!—and must ensure that our visit took full advantage of Mr Halle's orchestral performances and the various organ recitals scheduled throughout the day, which the Victorian child had circled in the much-handled programme.

I hadn't been to an art gallery myself since I was dragged there by my school, but I agreed to give it a go.

When we got into the city centre, I was amazed. The streets were full of them, Victorian children just like mine, each with a bemused parent trailing behind as they raced towards the gallery. I had no idea so many Victorian children existed; there were hundreds, and while we waited in the queue, I got talking to one of the other parents. He'd got his Victorian child from the same internet advert and was having the same trouble keeping it entertained. It was great to share my problems with another parent, and later that day, as we trooped home and I watched my Victorian child jabbering away with the other Victorian children about the paintings and the sculptures, I began to wonder whether I should read up about the behaviour of Victorian fathers. I could grow an elaborate moustache, perhaps invest in special wax. The idea appealed and, recalling one of the tunes from the organ recital, I began to whistle through my teeth, which the Victorian child said was a vulgar affectation and exceedingly annoying to the ear. It was then I realised that the child was middle-class and I went upstairs to look for the contract.

Heart Keeps Holding On

FROM SOMEWHERE IN the dark, the director's voice said 'Action' and Kirsty began her introduction, explaining the premise — haunted museums — with a significant dipping of her eyelashes over the phrase occult phenomenon every time the script brought it round.

'The original 1848 exhibition,' Kirsty oozed, 'generated many emotional charges within the Manchester community. We hope that tonight, at the reprise of the show here at Manchester Museum, some of those psychic ripples will be detected — with the help of spiritualist Garth Brando.'

The camera panned to Garth, leaning against the wall, hands tightly fisted, his tanned, wrinkly face quivering. With that sly, oily look in his eyes, Garth Brando had the appearance of a Z-list light entertainer, and until that week, I'd thought the man was nothing but a carnival showman. But this stuff is all about sides — this side and the other side — and when Garth Brando took me over to his side, things looked very different.

The camera glided from Garth to me. Bathed in infra-red, I would look like one of the very spectres the TV audience tuned-in for — eyes gleaming like hot little beads, whited-out face bloated and puckered as though I'd been crying.

'With me is communications manager, Angela.' Kirsty

continued. 'Angela, has there been any strange phenomenon around the exhibits?'

'Well, there's hasn't been much time so far, but—'

I stopped. Gareth Brando had gone into one of his spasms. His mouth had crinkled into an ugly gash and he had begun to gibber, sweat, and make wild, mindless gestures in the air. He was breathing as though he had been plunged into icy water. His famous altered state. I tried to move away, but he lunged and grabbed the lapels of my jacket. I could smell the peppery aftershave he spread everywhere like a spore of his personality.

He yelled into my face as if I was someone else entirely. 'Bobby, Bobby!' he cried, in strident stage-northern. 'This museum is better than a bloody puppy show! A bloody puppy show!'

The camera swooped up, down, round and about, mimicking the revolving eyes of a dozen ghosts.

Then Garth moaned long and low. 'Wait, wait. I'm getting something else. Something darker.'

All was silent but for the click of the cameraman's chewing gum.

Garth walked on mincing tiptoe towards a small side room. 'It's coming from here. Can you feel it? A terrible dread. A horrible fear. Miserable, desperate hours have been spent in this room.'

'That's where we carry out staff appraisals,' I said, attracting a sharp elbow from Kirsty.

'Something dark,' Garth said. 'A life, a young life. A young life tragically ended. Someone else is coming through. A woman. Someone's mother, I think.' Garth adopted an high wheedling northern tenor.' 'E was only nineteen ... snuffed out like a candle 'e was.' Garth's own voice again: 'Now I'm getting the letter T. I'm getting Tom. I'm getting Tommy.'

Cut to voice over and the story of Tommy Reagan, a young bricklayer who died erecting the original exhibition hall. Garth had read the papers I'd given him and learned them well. The filming was over and Kirsty thanked us — she had a powerful segment for the show.

The room was still dark when Garth encircled my waist with his arm. His upper-lip and tongue entrapped the lobe of my ear, sucking it in like a popsicle. Again he said he sensed something inside me, something we both understood.

I stood naked at the window of Garth Brando's room on the 29th floor of the Hilton Hotel, sipping cava and looking out over the city. Garth lay on the bed tapping the keys of his Blackberry, softly singing to the Frank Sinatra song drifting from his iPod speakers.

All of Manchester's dead were floating over the city. The sky bristled with a million dead souls, waiting for Garth Brando's call, eager to impart information from the other side and wishing that that there were more people like Garth Brando, people ready to listen and happy to help. Garth had shown me how to see them. There they were, flicking in and out of view, like bright little fish.

Garth was behind me. He cupped my breast with his hand and pressed himself against my back.

I turned and kissed his shoulder. 'I thought I would have to wait until I died for this.'

Domino Bones

YOU'RE AN ARCHAEOLOGIST, so you must work with bones, they always say and I say, not really, but that's exactly what I was doing back then; piecing together the skeleton of a fifteenth-century farmer who'd been found preserved in peat.

I had it laid out on a huge table like a jigsaw and I remember the sounds it made: the finger-joints chick-chicking together, the squeak of ink-drenched felt as I numbered the pieces with my special pen.

The university was next to a prison and while I worked I would look out of the window and watch the security vans coming and going. The vans would stand at the prison gate for ages, engines grumbling, while lengthy arrangements were made to allow the vehicles back inside. I would look at the vans, then at the dead farmer's bones, then back to the vans, and I would think of those trapped men, yearning for the brush of wind on their skin. I didn't know if they could see anything through the van's blackened windows, but one day I wrote some words in big letters on a piece of paper and held it up to the window. I held the paper there for a long time until the gates had been opened and the vans allowed in, and the next day I wrote down different words and did it again, and the next day, and the day after that. Every day I wrote new words on the paper and held it up as the vans waited, and after I'd finished and the vans had all gone, I returned to assembling the bones of the dead farmer who made a hollow plinking sound like dominos.

HALF LOVED

Some World, Somewhere

J EFF DIDN'T SMOKE, gave up years ago, but he missed the camaraderie, so when Luke invited him outside while he had a fag, Jeff quickly agreed, taking his cup of tea as something to do with his hands. The sun was scorching hot, so they huddled under a scrap of shade cast by the stunted birch sprouting from a crack in the pavement. Luke cupped a flame, put his cigarette to the fire and sucked tobacco, while Jeff sipped tea, envying the sensuous curl of smoke from Luke's nostrils.

Luke began, in his low, searching, cigarette-scratched voice, to talk to Jeff about man stuff. Was Jeff a man of the world?

Some world, somewhere, Jeff supposed.

How many different women had Jeff shagged? Round figures, nothing specific. Had Jeff ever had sex in an office or work environment? In a toilet? Were there any sexual acts Jeff hadn't tried? How tall was the tallest women Jeff had ever shagged? Who had been the most educationally qualified? What height had been the shortest girl? Who was the stupidest? The fattest?

Jeff replied in a careful, considered way and Luke nodded, pressing his lips together, saying: mmm, yes, I see, yet making no suggestions as to how Jeff might experience the same wild, untiring sex life as Luke, with its unending supply of differently shaped women from every social strata.

This part of his chat over, Luke butted out his cigarette on the concrete, ground it fiercely with his heel, lit another and, using the fag as a pointer, indicated a particular balcony on the new block of flats opposite. The new block had been thrown up in the past year and was a brutal collision of cones, spheres and rectangles, ruining the line of the streetscape and rendering illegible the handsome neo-gothic façade of the John Rylands library down the street. Jeff looked at the balcony indicated by Luke and after a few moments a young woman appeared wearing a dressing gown which, when she waved down at Luke, fell open flashing a strip of milky skin. Inky short hair framed an impish face.

Luke waved back and the woman tossed her head defiantly, mimed pantomime laughter, then leaned on the balcony, smoking, looking down at them with a vulpine grin.

Luke told Jeff that the woman was Claire's mother. Claire was Luke's girlfriend. One thing Jeff was certain of: this young lady looked like nobody's mother.

Claire's mother went inside and reappeared with a dining table, which she placed on the balcony. She then produced a deckchair, which she lifted on to the table, positioning it carefully so that it wouldn't slide off, and she climbed onto the elaborate structure and sat down. This way she could view the city over the opaque glass screen that prevented residents tumbling off. It was, after all, the fifteenth floor.

Luke's face was glossy with sweat. He drew in a long

draught of smoke, his cheeks sinking into deep hollows and a faint whistle coming from his teeth, then asked Jeff, though a smile shaped for and aimed at Claire's mother, if in Jeff's opinion it would be all right to see a mother and a daughter at the same time.

'What do mean, see?'

'You know, see.'

Jeff looked up at Claire's mother. She was wearing headphones and her head twitched to and fro while her foot, dangling over the balcony rail, tapped a rapid beat in the air.

Jeff worried about whether he was getting into another pink/brown snooker ball scenario, which was, in his opinion, disgusting.

'I'm not sure, Luke,' Jeff said, secretly thinking that the last thing a man should do is betray his girlfriend with his girlfriend's mother. But then again, Jeff wasn't as experienced with women as Luke, so he kept this opinion to himself.

Luke had a sly way of smiling that allowed little wisps of cigarette smoke to escape from between his almost-closed lips, and he was doing that while he looked up at the woman on the balcony. He explained what he knew about the mother and daughter's relationship. It turned out they didn't get on. They'd had some row over the mother's last boyfriend, so there was hardly any contact between them. Luke knew this was the mother from pictures, and he knew she lived in this block. That's why he had began to take his fag breaks on that side of the building. Curiosity. To see what she looked like, this ogre, this hated woman. As he explained this to Jeff, Luke became increasingly agitated. He abhorred the fact that Claire wouldn't even come to the phone when her own mother rang, and that letters with her own mother's handwriting on the envelope—her own mother's handwriting—went straight into the bin. But the main thing Jeff had to understand was this. Luke took a long, deep pull on his fag. He was developing a little thing for Claire's mother. More than little, really. He'd had a few drinks with her. And the woman had no idea that Luke was her daughter's boyfriend. Luke thought at first that he would just find out what the lady was like. Maybe try to get her and her mum back together. It wasn't right, a family split up like that. But after he'd met her a few times, he forgot to mention about the daughter. And the more often he saw her, the more difficult it became to bring such a thing up. She had, Luke explained, these faraway eyes. He let this fact land, and neither of the men said anything for a long time. Luke pouted and exhaled smoke from the side of his mouth with a brusque malignance. They were both thinking about the faraway eyes.

Jeff looked up at the woman again. Long white legs on the balcony rail, slick with sun tan oil, glistening in the light. Faraway eyes. Jeff wondered if there was a scientific explanation for faraway eyes.

Luke explained that he was, by nature, a big sharer, and he wondered if it was morally acceptable to allow the two women to share him. What did Jeff think? Should he do it?

'I'm not sure, Luke. It's going to have to be your call.'

'Have you ever done anything like that?'

'Not exactly like that, no.'

'No. I guess not.'

Jeff thought privately that it would be simpler if Luke had started seeing the mother first. Then there would be no way even Luke could consider seeing the daughter, because she'd be like his stepdaughter. But the other way round? Jeff wasn't sure.

Luke read this thought.

'I mean, its not like I met the mother first. It's not like it's sick. Is it? I mean, is it? Is it sick, Jeff? That's what I need to know?'

'I really don't know, Luke.'

Claire's mum went inside and emerged again with a cocktail glass of green liquid, a red paper umbrella sticking out of it. She sipped audaciously, pinky finger cocked; Luke and Jeff were at work and she wasn't.

'Look at her. She is fucking gorgeous. Why is Claire so nasty to her?'

'Families,' Jeff said. 'It's like that sometimes.'

'She's like a mother-in-law, I suppose. And mother-in-laws are like stepmothers. They don't love like real mothers. Always evil.' Luke chucked his fag onto the ground and stamped it out. He seemed to be churning inside with unhappy lust. 'Everyone knows about stepmothers, Jeff. Or didn't you get fairy stories in that home?'

Luke waved up to Claire's mother, pointed at his wrist and mouthed later, then squeezed Jeff's shoulder roughly in his fingers and said, 'Thanks for listening, mate,' before disappearing inside.

Why did Luke always have to mention the home? Whatever Luke discussed with Jeff, the home ended up relevant in some way.

Jeff stayed to finish his tea and Claire's mother sat back more comfortably on her deckchair, crossed her legs, and allowed one slim foot to slip part way out of its sandal. She sipped her drink, tapped her toes, bopped her head.

Her mobile trilled and Jeff watched her reach down, pick it up and cradle it against her ear. She chatted happily for a time until abruptly she jerked up out of her seat and began to prowl the balcony, head shaking alarmingly, arms flinging this way and that, fingers jabbing at invisible enemies, mouth rattling staccato sentences into the phone. Jeff waited for something to happen.

Which it did. She screamed and tossed the phone off the balcony and it smacked against the concrete in front of him, fragments of metal and plastic spinning off. Then she heaved herself onto the balcony rail and sat astride it, wobbling drunkenly.

Jeff called out to her, but she didn't hear. Headphones on, she sat on the rail, swaying and gyrating, glass in one hand, fag in the other.

Should he call the police? Or Luke? The woman could plummet down at any moment and crack into the concrete, smashing into pieces like her phone. He called out again, but still no response. Maybe he was worrying unnecessarily. Maybe she did this sort of thing all the time. But he couldn't help thinking of her daughter Claire, and how, despite her mother's antics, she must surely love her really and how happy they both could be if Luke was somehow off the scene, and possibly there was a part for Jeff in all of this.

Then from Claire's balcony came a long impossible moan and Jeff set off running, kicking a piece of broken mobile phone out of the way as he went.

The Next Best Thing

MIDGE URE BROUGHT us together. Not many people can say that. We met in the foyer at the Shire Hall, both of us buying a single ticket to see Midge, and we joked about all the old lags, has-beens and never-beens on tour and playing places like Howden Shire Hall. You said you were in Howden for a couple of days on Press Association business, so anything was better than staring at the hotel telly. You used to like Ultravox, but rated them more in the John Foxx days, before Midge joined.

We bumped into each other again at the bar before Midge went on. They didn't have real ale, so you said you'd have Guinness as it was the next best thing, and I had that too. There were many more gigs after that first night. Many more has-beens and never-beens. Every few weeks you had a meeting up here at the Press Association. There was never any warning, but I didn't mind. We'd get tickets to some old lag at the Shire Hall, we'd drink the next best thing, and the following day we'd picnic in the Minster graveyard on your lunch break. I knew there was nothing permanent on the cards, but I did expect some minimum standards. A text on my birthday. A call when my mother was in hospital. Some sort of message on Christmas day.

Guinness was our theme and I began to steal a Guinness glass every time we had a date. We'd laugh about it on the way back to your room, and talk about the next best thing. In the end, I had a Guinness glass for nearly all of our dates and I lined them up on my window ledge as a public display, a display only you and I would understand.

I don't touch the Guinness glasses now. Never move them, never clean them. There are thirteen. They have gathered a lot of dust, but I don't think I should interfere with nature. I like to see them in a row, dust and cobwebs piling up, because they remind me of different times, times when a man from the Press Association would take me to see Hazel O'Connor, or Chris Difford from Squeeze, or that one out of The Stranglers, and we'd drink the next best thing and watch the latest has-been and laugh about the eighties. What was so great about the eighties, anyway? Everything was artificial. There was nothing warm about the decade, nothing worth remembering at all.

Portraits of Insane Women

WARREN READ IN a men's magazine he picked up at the barbers that art galleries are perfect for picking up women. This fact surprised him because his entire working life had been in art galleries, and he'd had no idea. He'd met his wife Georgina in a gallery — that's where they had both worked — but the fact that people used Warren's carefully curated spaces to feed explosive, untiring sex lives appalled him. His efforts to waken the soul with the tender strokes of art were wasted. Years of registering, ticketing, cataloguing, placing, interpreting, caring, protecting meant nothing. The public didn't want his art. They wanted secret nooks for fleshy encounters. Soft chairs, heavy curtains, peepholes — tissues, even. His art gallery was a pick-up joint and Warren, a pimp.

But Georgina had run away. With Vernon, a wedding photographer. And although he'd tried the bachelor life for a few weeks, without her, without Georgina, without a woman, his life was dingy and meaningless. Georgina's last email spurred him to do something about it. YOUR VACUOUS CHIMP-SCRAWL MAKES MY EYES VOMIT, she pounded out in fat capitals. Where had she learned this language? It can't have come from Vernon, the quiet wedding photographer, who specialised in novelty poses for his couples (his *Pulp Fiction* set-up was very popular). Warren had no bad feelings towards Vernon. He'd never met him, but he'd walked past the man's studio a few times and once glimpsed him arranging a family portrait and using a puppet to make the children laugh.

Warren wanted to stop doing furtive things, like watching Vernon using puppets to make children laugh. Warren wanted forward movement, and a new woman would give him this. And if Warren couldn't pick up a woman in a gallery, then who could? Manchester Art Gallery's new show about Victorian collections seemed an appropriate populist choice; many single, available women would be wandering unsupervised. All he needed was the nerve and the blood.

At first he couldn't concentrate on hunting out women because he was so appalled at the poor quality of the hang: the schools of Sienna, Arezzo and Florence were chaotically jumbled together and ascribed in a slap dash fashion. Eventually, however, he spotted an interesting woman; slim, somewhere in her thirties, and with ginger hair, which made her seem more attainable. Her nose was small and turned-up at the end. He decided to make his move in the photography section, where she was narrowing her eyes in intense concentration before a landscape by Gustav Legney. Warren imagined their gazes as beams of torch light, mingling in front of the photograph, and felt suddenly exposed and tiny. Words swelled like a bubble in his chest and he thought he would never free them. Then he remembered the advice in the magazine at the barber's: Offer your feelings about the art work, then reveal something personal.

'Did you realise,' Warren blurted, 'that the sky and sea parts of this image would have had to be exposed completely separately, then stitched together?' Adding quickly, 'It reminds me of my father.'

The woman pressed her lips together and widened her eyes, nodding slowly. 'Did you father expose himself?'

'Expose himself? No, no.'

She broke out in squeaking little laughter. 'No I didn't mean — I'm sorry. I mean did he expose pictures? Was he a photographer?'

'No, he was a grocer. I'm Warren, by the way.'

'Becky.'

Becky looked at Warren's face, then down to his shoes, which must have confirmed something because she made a darting fish movement with her hand and a whoosh sound with her mouth, indicating they should overtake the couple in front and move on to the next picture — Rylander's *Two Ways of Life*.

Warren and Becky were looking at art together. They were behaving like a couple. This was easy.

Rylander's *Two Ways Of Life* was made up of 36 separate negatives, stitched together in the way Vernon digitally merged different images to make the novelty film stills for his newly weds. The photograph had been controversial in 1857, as it depicted orgiastic scenes involving bare breasted women. Warren worried Becky would ask him which way of life he would prefer, and as he would be inclined to say a little of both, he hoped to God she had read the same book about picking people up in galleries and knew to avoid direct questioning.

'Sometimes I feel,' said Becky, 'that my life is lots of separate exposures blended together. No unity. It's like I am seeing the world through a giant fly's eye with lots of different octagonal viewpoints.'

'I know what you mean,' Warren said, unable to imagine what she was talking about.

The next display was a set of medical photos called *Portraits of Insane Women*, images that seemed to Warren exploitative and made him feel greasy. But Becky liked them more than anything else.

'Look at their faces. In those days people knew how to be insane. You had proper mad people. Do you remember how street people used to mutter? You don't get that now. What happened to muttering? It was like a different language — burbling, rasping, full of passion and grit. I used to like to hear them muttering. When I was a kid, a woman used to follow me round the supermarket softly singing and tittering. Another used to swear. Where are they now?'

She bent her neck for a new angle. 'You can see she is authentically deranged. The hollowness behind the eyes, the twisting of the mouth. Mad people have very thick hair, have you noticed? Do you think they have special shampoo? In asylums?'

Warren was concerned about her attitude to the insane women, but he felt that these attitudes were something he could work on. He was out there now. You had to work with the materials you were given. That was another thing the magazine in the barber's said.

In the café, Becky and Warren talked about their lives. She had recently broken-up with her boyfriend and had been visiting the gallery for months. Warren was the first normal person she'd got chatting to, so when he proposed his plan, she was happy to agree.

At Vernon's photography studio, Warren and Becky flicked though the pose book. Vernon had many of the necessary costumes but, if needs be, he could simply knock up the whole thing digitally. It was up to them. Warren, however, was prepared. He showed Becky the film poster for forties film noir Gun Crazy and she agreed right away; the gaze in the woman's eyes was exactly like one of the portraits of insane women at the gallery.

Georgina would be amazed when she saw Warren with this red-haired girl in high heels and short skirt, breasts bursting out of a tight green sweater, pointing a handgun at the viewer, with Warren behind her, cigarette drooping, a fugitive look on his face, his eyes exposing a vacant soul whose only mission was the ruthless pursuit of pleasure.

Monkeys in Love

AFTER THE FOLK mass, it was usual for Father Rafferty to let the marmoset out of its cage. The congregation loved to see Starsy scampering up the stained glass windows. But the minute Starsy was out, he always lunged straight for whatever young woman Father Rafferty was interested in at that time, as if he were following some invisible chemical dotted line. Father Rafferty recognised the beginnings of it today when Starsy was making lewd gestures through his bars at Petra who played the musical saw in the folk group.

The folk group was the nurturing ground for all Father Rafferty's new friends. 'It's modern folk,' he would say. 'You don't have to put your finger in your ear.'

The sobbing notes from Petra's musical saw were still hanging in the air as Father Rafferty undid the lock to Starsy's cage and, as expected, the marmoset shot out over a dozen rows of pews and jumped on Petra's head, tugging her hair, going *ee ee ee*.

Father Rafferty raced over. 'Come on, Starsy, off, off! Leave Petra alone!' and Petra smiled in a frozen, horrified way as if she knew the marmoset was some kind of priest avatar. Father Rafferty thought back to Petra bowing her saw, her face screwed up in puzzlement and joy as she reached for notes whose exquisite out-of-tuneness summed-up all of his feelings about her. Her woollen saw case lay crumpled on the floor like the skin of a snake. He knew Petra wouldn't return to the folk group and had a suspicion that she might even give up playing the musical saw, throwing away all of what he loved, all of what was deep and holy in her.

Later that week, Father Rafferty was standing on the deck of a cross-Channel ferry. He tied the top of a big sack very tightly with nylon twine. It was heavy, with the big rock in there as well, but he managed to drag it to the edge, heft it up over the rails, and drop it in. A scarf of froth remained on the surface for a few seconds, then quickly it was gone and there was no sign it had ever been there.

He could see land on the other side. In Germany he'd meet another girl, just like Petra. Maybe she'd play a musical instrument too, but not a bowed instrument this time, maybe brass, maybe a trombone in an oompah band. It's still folk music, a type of folk music. Folk music just means music for the people, it covers a lot of different things.

Is Your Thought Really Necessary?

M R FLEMING'S HOUSE was a tiny white cube, nearly empty of possessions, in which Mr Fleming lounged on a white sofa in white pyjamas and white paper slippers; a weightless, purified lifestyle achieved only by complete abstinence from active thought.

He poured two glasses of water into sparkling, antiseptically-clean glasses.

'The presentation is tomorrow?'

Harold nodded.

'Well, pup, stop them thinking. That's all you have to do. The stretch is a 10% reduction and the government would love, love, love to see it achieved in Wigan. Our disposal sites are almost full, and the Standish ward is a re-change area. PowerPoint, I take it?'

'Yes.'

Harold took a sip of water so cold it made his eyeballs hurt.

'Be careful, pup. PowerPoint. I looked it up. It has a reputation for stimulating thought. And causing additional thought is the opposite of what we require.'

'I've delivered a thousand PowerPoint presentations and I've never excited anyone to original thought yet.'

Mr Fleming nodded towards Harold's thought-sac, 'Don't forget to empty your sac before your presentation.'

It was three-quarters full and still inflating.

'Your mind has been very active. Thought-free is care-free.'

Harold winced at the well-worn motto.

'And pup? During the presentation, don't laugh. People off the floor tell me your laugh is infectious. Kind of bubbles, they say. Now, pup, go and stop those bastards thinking!'

Halfway down the path from Mr Fleming's village, Harold stopped. He could see the lights of Standish, hear the chittering of voices, the throb of music, the thrum of tyres on roads; this was the sound of thinking, a complex drone that hung like a pall over every thoughtful part of town. Further along, he could see the thought-dump, the articulated arm of a digger's shovel silhouetted against the moon as it heaped up thought-sacs for compacting and burial.

He looked back towards the dozens of white cubes on the hill, each identical to the next, and spotted Mr Fleming's dark shape at the window, the glass of water in his hand glinting. In the next cube was another shadow, and in the next, and in the next. Nearly every manager lived in the white cubes above town, and they all knew Harold's presentation to the Standish Local Area Forum was tomorrow. Harold continued down the hill, leaving the sugar-cube houses behind him, aware of each manager watching, attempting to discern from Harold's gait whether he was the one who would free the town from excessive thought.

At home Harold opened up PowerPoint.

IS YOUR THOUGHT REALLY NECESSARY?

A PRESENTATION TO STANDISH COMMUNITY
LOCAL AREA FORUM ON THOUGHT AVOIDANCE
AND THOUGHT RECYCLING.

HAROLD PLAIN
TARGET MANAGER, ENVIRONMENT TEAM
WIGAN LOCAL STRATEGIC PARTNERSHIP
WIGAN'S STRETCH TARGET AND HOW STANDISH
CAN PLAY A PART.
REDUCING UNNEEDED THOUGHT IN WIGAN
BY 10 %

He wondered about using some funny clip art, maybe some expanding thought-sacs, which grew so full people floated away, or the one where a thought-sac explodes, scattering innermost thoughts all over the town, random people picking them up and laughing. But those jokes were old.

He thought about his performance. What was it Mr Fleming had said about his laugh? What was wrong with his laugh? He tried to laugh, to see what it sounded like, but who could laugh on demand?

He would begin by reminding the Standish Local Area Forum of the basic facts:

THOUGHT IS SOLID MATTER AND WEIGHS
APPROXIMATELY 150 GRAMS PER SQUARE 10CM

Harold was safe with these facts. They were well known, and would not cause excessive thought amongst the audience. He switched from PowerPoint and clicked onto his

new favourite website: www.lookwhosbeenthinkinga-
boutyou.com:

*THOUGHT IS MADE FROM AN AMALGAM OF FAT
AND HAIR FOLLICLES A LITTLE LIKE FINGERNAILS.*

Use of this website was prohibited for Council workers.
Whether it was legal or illegal to buy and sell thoughts was
a grey area.

THOUGHTS ARE 78% WATER

But it was definitely not the done thing for someone in
Harold's position to even look, never mind register. Harold
had gone one further.

*THE AVERAGE PERSON PRODUCES 300 GRAMS OF
SOLID THOUGHT A DAY*

He had bought a thought and it was sitting there on his
desk.

*THE SHINY PATINA THAT COATS A FRESHLY
PRODUCED THOUGHT IS A SPECIAL MUCOUS SCI-
ENTISTS BELIEVE EVOLVED TO PROTECT OUR
THOUGHTS FROM ANIMAL CONSUMPTION.*

He had searched for his name, the date and time he was
interested in, and got a strong result from the town where
he was brought up:

WE ENJOY WATCHING OTHER PEOPLE'S THOUGHTS BEING EXTRUDED, EVEN THOUGH WE DON'T KNOW WHAT EACH THOUGHT IS ABOUT.

The seller had photographed the thought alluringly, posed against a velvet drape; he had to have it.

WE ARE FASCINATED BY THE VARIETY IN THE SIZE AND SHAPE OF THOUGHTS.

He fingered the thought absently. This was a thought someone had had about Harold. It squatted like a stone — inert, inscrutable, yielding nothing. What had the thought been about? How long had it lasted? A label gave the time, date and location, but nothing else was known. It was encased in resin and, turning it, he could see every aspect, a small bronze-coloured lozenge floating in the centre of the plastic casing.

MANY PSEUDO-SCIENCES HAVE DEVELOPED BASED AROUND THE STUDY OF THE COLOUR AND SHAPE OF THOUGHTS, BUT NONE OF THESE THEORIES HAVE GAINED CREDENCE WITH MEDICAL EXPERTS.

He'd bought it because he suspected it related to the very moment when he had asked Hilary Meldrum out for a date, and this was what she had been thinking when she'd turned him down.

He searched the website again for any other thoughts Hilary Meldrum might have had, but nothing came up. He returned to his presentation.

The aim of Wigan partnership stretch target was, Mr

Fleming said, to reduce the volume of thought in Standish to a thin stream, rather than this clonking machine-gun rattle of one heavy thought after another. But Harold couldn't express it in that way. He decided to give the Standish Local Area Forum more facts.

THERE ARE 27 THOUSAND THOUGHT-FILL SITES ALL OVER THE COUNTRY, AND CAPACITY IS NOW ONLY 85%.
IF WE CONTINUE TO THINK AT THE CURRENT RATE THE CONSEQUENCES ARE DIRE.

The problem was that all of these ideas would make them think, and that was the opposite of what Mr Fleming and the other partnership managers wanted him to achieve.

STANDISH IS ONE OF THE MOST THOUGHTFUL AREAS IN THE COUNTRY, WITH RESIDENTS THINK-ING ON AVERAGE THREE TIMES MORE OFTEN, FOUR TIMES MORE DEEPLY AND HAVING TWICE THE AVERAGE VARIETY OF THOUGHTS.

It was a vicious circle. How could he stimulate these people to come up with imaginative ways to stop thinking, without encouraging them to use their imaginations?

To stop thinking. The most powerful people in the world were those who had evolved to have no need to think at all. Up on the hills, in their tiny white houses with no televisions, no books, no games, nothing, not even relationships, lived these uber-evolved humans, looking down with disdain as the thought collection trucks again began their rounds.

The phone went. It was Mr Fleming.

'How's it going, pup?'

'Not bad. Getting there. All but the formatting.'

'Ping it across then, Pup, and I'll cast my old owl eye over it.'

He was about to send the presentation to Mr Fleming and reached across to plug in the broadband cable when, in his haste, he knocked his precious resin-encased thought on to the stone floor where it bounced a few times before landing up against the wall. He picked it up and noticed the casing was cracked. He sniffed—a fusty, fecund smell, something old, intense, and oddly resonant. He wondered: could he ingest it, somehow? Could he unravel its meaning?

He smashed the casing open against the edge of the table and placed the precious bronze lozenge on a piece of tissue. He'd never touched a thought before—you were advised not to when you were small—germs, danger, taboo. Yet he felt no fear. The thought was hard and dusty. In the kitchen he found the grater and made a pyramid of thought shreds on a saucer. He rolled it with tobacco, lit it, and took a long pull. As the smoke entered his lungs, he felt a light tingling all over his body. Gradually, the thought crept up through his blood and into his head.

That's when he felt it. He now knew what Hilary Meldrum had really thought.

Harold, he's OK she said in her unmistakeable West Country accent, but it's just his laugh. And then he heard his own laugh as reproduced by Hilary Meldrum in her thoughts, exaggerated, higher and repeated several times. There was no doubt.

This was Hilary Meldrum thinking about his laugh.

He took another long pull on his thought cigarette.

And he heard her thinking again, saying his laugh was

fake, it was a fake laugh. A fake laugh. That's all it was. A fake laugh. The people on the floor had said it kind of bubbled.

He looked out of his window, up to the white sugar cube house where Mr Fleming in his white robes and paper slippers was waiting for him to ping the draft across. He decided to insert some stimulating material for the people of the Standish Local Area Forum. He would make them laugh and make himself laugh too. He needed the practice.

HALF WHOLE

The Valued Coach Driver and his Spiral Wife

PETER WON'T GO into Ikea with Natalie because he hates the spiral. He prefers a grid. You know where you are with a grid. You can change your mind and do something else. A spiral is a one-way street: forwards, backwards, a binary way of progressing. Fine for single-celled creatures, but Peter is a coach driver and coach drivers like to think they are capable of more in the world than just following a spiral from its outer arm into its centre and then back out again. Imagine if Peter took his coach passengers on spiral routes. Imagine towns as spirals. He couldn't bear to think about it.

Natalie likes spirals, Peter likes grids. He and Natalie visualise everything in completely different ways. For example, Peter visualises the calendar year as a straight line from January to December, whereas Natalie pictures it as a circle. Natalie likes a lot of other spiral-shaped things as well as IKEA. Ferns, shells, flowers. She was even interested in a spiral-shaped bone from an animal's ear she came across in a museum.

'What about your precious vinyl,' Natalie once said. 'Isn't it all made of spirals?'

He had no answer to this. She was right. Without the spiral, there would be no Beatles, no Stones, no Bowie.

'Perhaps,' he said to her, 'records made using a grid will be the next big thing. Records designed to jump, to play different tunes every time. It's not just the spiral, anyway, there is something fascist about Ikea. The Allen key looks like a swastika.'

'And did we have to come on the coach?' she moaned.

'You know the deal,' he reminded her. 'We bring the coach, I get my lunch for a penny. That's the special deal for valued coach drivers.'

'But your uniform, as well? On your day off?'

'You're not complaining at lunch for a penny, are you?' he said.

They ate meatballs and chips, then Peter went back to the coach and Natalie headed off into the dizzying spiral aisles of the yellow and blue monster. Peter sat in his coach and looked at the road. The road to Ikea resembled a road to the future. Wide and empty with tidy, manicured edges, flanked by glass buildings in copses of trees. A fountain sparkled in the sun. He imagined everyone in this Ikea future would be bald, even the women, and they would wear black, shiny, knee-length boots, fitted tightly to the calves.

Natalie returned half an hour later and seemed upset. She hadn't even bought anything.

'I'm upset,' she said. 'I haven't even bought anything. I found a break in the spiral. A wormhole. It was in the middle of the inner spiral arm, in shelving, disguised behind a CD rack. It's the route staff use to get through the shop without having to follow the spiral. That's the thing. You don't have to follow the spiral. The wormhole takes a straight line through every spiral corridor and out to the tills. It was like,' she twisted the top off her bottle of water and took a long gulp, 'discovering a new dimension. Customers can use it,' she went on. 'There's nothing to stop them. Now I know it's there, I know I will use it if I'm in a hurry. And I don't like it. I don't know what to do, Peter.'

Peter stared ahead through the window of his coach. He was regretting rearranging the furniture at home into a spiral shape as a surprise, and was trying to work out how he could get home before her and put it back to the way it was.

Music Like Ours
Never Dies

MARION SAID THE article could have been written with me in mind, and I riffled through the supplement and there it was: Losing it — The Bay City Rollers' Story.

The Rollers had everything, but threw it all away. They were egos on legs, emotionally cramped, and their manager had a sinister, seamy undertow that eventually destroyed them.

Marion was right. Their story was our story. I was self-obsessed, vain, and paid slipshod attention to Marion's needs. The Bay City Rollers were encoded in me. And the manager? He was my father. Emotions were unsilted and my tears fell on Les McKeon's face. When Marion returned from her run, I hugged her close.

'Darling, I will never allow us to become the Bay City Rollers.'

She tssskd and flipped Les over. 'This is the article I meant.'

Emotional Infidelity, it said, above a picture of a man and woman on a park bench.

Alone, I drew a penis jutting out of the man's trousers and a moustache on the woman. That's what the Rollers would have done. What matters is the moment, not ever-lasting fame.

The Buddy Holly Electrician

I DON'T KNOW WHAT we were arguing about when you threw the bowl, but I remember ducking just in time, which was a good job judging by the speed it whooshed over my head, disgorging a comet's tail of cereal behind it before smashing into the wall with a clang of porcelain that reverberated in the silence. I remember us standing there, looking at the mess on the wall and floor, before bursting into laughter, kissing, then making love on that old, scratchy sofa. Afterwards we lay in each other's arms, looking up at the splashes and curls of cereal that had formed a teeming many-armed galaxy on the wall. You asked me if I would clean the mess up, and I said yes, but I couldn't help thinking it was unfair — you'd thrown the bowl, yet I had to clean up.

The next morning you weren't angry when I showed you how I had left the bowl lying where it fell and had hoovered carefully around it. You just laughed, and we hugged and made love again on the scratchy sofa. For the first time in years, we felt complete.

We were both pointlessly, stupidly stubborn, always had been. We knew that neither of us would ever clean up the bowl. It stayed exactly where it had fallen. Sometimes we hid it with a piece of furniture, often we didn't bother. We joked it was an installation and we were looking for Arts Council funding. By Christmas, the upturned cereal bowl was part of the house. The smell was gone, the puddle of cereal had become a hard, brown splodge, and it looked festive with tinsel trailed around and a bauble on top. It was the best Christmas we'd had. We didn't row once. It was as if our sour, curdled love had been drained away and replaced with a sweet and pure liquid. And all because of the bowl.

All this time we knew that if we disturbed the bowl, a stream of demons would rush out to infect us and later that year we were proved right, when a young electrician who, in his thick black spectacles looked a bit like Buddy Holly, had to crawl under the floor boards to rewire the house. We'd rolled the bowl up inside the carpet and put it safely in the hall, but the Buddy Holly electrician thought we wanted to throw the old carpet away.

So he took it to a landfill refuge tip where it was crushed and buried.

When we realised what the Buddy Holly electrician had done, we sat there. The raw, fabulous silence. The shock. Something malevolent growing around us. We breathed a foul atmosphere on the edge of explosion.

We didn't hold it against the Buddy Holly electrician. We allowed him to complete the job and after a while noticed that having the Buddy Holly electrician around had the same affect as the bowl. It seemed he had inherited its powers.

We listened to his words as he told his wife on the phone that he would have to stay a little longer, and I remember you wrote down the things he said on a piece of paper which you rolled up and put away in your pocket. I cleared out a cupboard for his electrical tools while you helped him unwrap a new toothbrush and showed him up to the bathroom. We listened outside the spare room to the rustle of him removing his trousers and the thunk of his belt buckle hitting the floor. Having an electrician around the place would be useful. There were many jobs he could get stuck into. He'd always have plenty to do.

Keep Them On, Love

'IF YOU SQUEEZE your eyes together and jiggle the string, it looks like a real aquarium.' She pulled the cord and made the plastic fish curtain dance and wondered whether Gareth would be watching from his window opposite.

Everyone kept coming back to the fact that she had kept her shoes on. The whole family thought keeping her shoes on was a big mistake. But they had blown it out of proportion. She really wanted it hung up in the bedroom, not in the hall. She'd hung it in the hall just to show it off. After all, it had cost five hundred quid, with the session and the printing and the frame. She never imagined they'd be so horrified. Especially the boys. It was tasteful. She was fifty, but she didn't look it in that picture, no one could say she looked fifty. The photographer was a real artist, he'd done a brilliant job. He'd advised her on the pose, he'd suggested she keep her shoes on.

She can't believe Gareth left her because of a photograph. The whole town was talking, he'd said. She'd been the answer to a question in the pub quiz.

So Gareth left and she got the goldfish for the office, as a joke, really. What'll you do when Gareth's gone? Get a goldfish. Similar memory and about as much use in the bedroom. And she'd done it, she'd bought a fish. Because that's how she behaved now. If she thought about something, she did it. She was fifty.

But Gareth also worked for the council and he told the office coordinator and you weren't allowed live creatures, so Goldie was taken away. She knew Gareth could see her office window from his desk. He could see the new fish curtain, the plastic coloured fish. And every time he looked across he'd be reminded how pathetic he was.

'Of course, why ever not?' she'd said when the photographer asked her back for some demonstration shots. She didn't even mind her photo being in his shop window. People pay attention to what's in a window. People stop and think, minds are changed, and now and again, they go inside.

What You See is There

MINKY LOVED BUILDINGS more than people. She claimed something grew between people and buildings and Sid pictured this substance as a type of crud, like the crud the design champion said the builders reamed from the wrinkles in the oak block floors in the art college.

'This design champion,' Minky said to Sid, while the design champion was off sorting out the hard hats, 'describe his looks.'

'Adequate,' Sid said

'Describe, not measure. What's his face like when he talks?'

'When he said crud, he pouted like Mick Jagger. He has pouty energy.'

A ripple of mockery or regret, he didn't know which, passed across her face.

'Stop staring at my face.'

'I'm not,' said Sid.

He was, though.

'Is he bleeding edge?' said Minky

'The bleediest,' Sid said.

The city council's bleeding edge design champion was giving Sid and Minky a tour of the half-refurbished art college so that Minky could write an article, and Sid was being Minky's eyes. He wasn't doing very well. He described the high windows sunk into the walls, but couldn't remember the term for the shape of the recesses. He told her about the wooden archways with carved leaves, but didn't know what kind of leaf. He told her about the shiny bricks that looked like tiles.

'Yes, yes, yes,' she said. 'Vitreous coated.'

A good description of masonry could make Minky's face light up like love, but Sid could never find the words, and it was sad to watch her tire and retreat as she grew bored with his efforts. Since she lost her sight, she no longer seemed able to disguise the feelings that passed across her face, and patches of pink rippled under her skin.

They stopped in a narrow, curving corridor, with light streaming in from a door at the far end. Leprous paint was peeling off the walls like birch skin.

'This is my favourite space,' the design champion said. His voice was soft and seemed to float like dandelion down. 'Look at the way it curves. There are no straight lines in nature.'

Sid felt trapped in a broken-off vein of the building, going nowhere and connected to nothing. 'Buildings thwart us constantly,' the design champion cooed. 'They are at war with time and always lose. Yet, some buildings, like this one, seem to flow with time, flow with us. Come out here.'

They followed him into the corridor. 'Feel this.' He took Minky's hands and pressed them against a wall cupboard. 'To understand buildings, you must collide with them.' Minky ran her fingers all over the cupboard — the locks, the knobs, the hinges — and her eyes went googly as she processed the shapes. 'That cupboard is listed,' the design champion explained. 'It's a listed cupboard.'

Sid wasn't thinking about the listed cupboard. He was thinking about the book he'd been reading to Minky the night before. He read to her every night. Sometimes esoteric volumes about urban design: 'Bodies are absent in architecture, but they remain architecture's unspoken condition.' Minky sighing, 'That's so true. Don't you agree, Sid?' But for relaxation it was chick lit—fat paperbacks with pink, embossed covers and script-font titles as if it was a diary scribbled into an exercise book. He had become interested in the adventures of Rosie, the heroine of Rosie Grows, and instead of noting the architectural points of interest in the art college, he was wondering whether the laconic carpenter Rosie met at the photography class would be at the end-of-term party. Rosie was funny and sad and made good jokes and got drunk and deserved something good to happen to her. He couldn't believe how the men in the book had lied and wondered whether he, Sid, was failing as a man in the way he devoted himself to making Minky happy.

A few weeks after she'd lost her sight, they went into the town centre and Minky asked Sid to describe everything. He told her about a woman in tight trousers moving naked mannequins about, but she interrupted.

'Tell me about things I would have noticed.'

It wasn't easy. Minky wanted to know about the clothes people wore, the hairstyles, the prices of things in windows, the colours of leaves, how people looked at each other, what litter could be seen, the expressions on shopkeepers' faces, whether people looked happy.

He had to read magazines to her, too.

'Ahem, Ahem. Now then. Contents: Toy boy cured my cancer, Kerry Katona's alcohol test, Orgasm boot camp, Terrorised by anorexic extremists, MWAH MWAH New York fashion . . .' but she stopped him mid-flow.

'Flip through the pages from the back. Give me headlines and pictures. For Christ's sake, Sid, all these years I have been your aerial, a sat-nav through the emotional world. I had no idea how lacking in receptors you were. Try harder, Sid, please. What I see is what you let me see.'

Room followed room followed room followed room and there were few features of interest. Here was the slate staircase which bore the scoops, bevels and indentations of a thousand footsteps. Here the famous wrought-iron stair gate that divided the art school from the rest of the building, the words school of art, spelled out in the metal. 'You don't say,' Minky said.

Minky was ravenous for descriptions of every physical space, but there were so many things in Sid's field of vision, he couldn't decide what to say. There was no end to seeing. If we do nothing else, we see. Like in *Clockwork Orange* where they pin your eyelids back.

In the old art room was a set of lockable pigeon holes; long, slim doors covering deep recesses into the wall where the art students used to store portfolios. Trudy's glass, said one, be careful. Others things had been scribbled on the wall. Revolution is the festival of the oppressed, and someone had drawn an arrow pointing to this saying, bollocks, evolution is the engine of the hog. A dartboard had been drawn on one wall, with life options written in the score areas — Dole, Go to poly, Heroin, Married with Kids, Religious Freak, Insanity. On a cardboard box was scribbled a chart of the builder's daily lives showing various mishaps.

'Are you reading, Sid? I can hear you reading.'

'Some stuff the builders have written. It says Harry gets gang bummed.'

Having exhausted the interior of the building, the design champion took the lift downstairs to fetch the key to the tasting garden and asked them to wait.

'Does he have nice clothes?' Minky said, when he was out of earshot.

'He's in a high-viz jacket, like us.'

'You like saying that word, don't you? High-viz. Makes you feel manly.'

'High-viz. High-viz.' Two builders walked by. carrying a roll of cable. and one nodded hello at Sid.

'I didn't know you had so little to say about buildings,' Minky said. 'But I've noticed you do like to say, rip it all out and start again. You often say that.'

'I like the idea.'

'You do, don't you? Well it's more subtle than that. It's all about layers, these refurbishments. An old building is like a palimpsest. Say palimpsest, Sid.'

'You know I won't say that word. It's a cissy word. Makes my lips purse up.'

'What would Rosie out of Rosie Grows do if she met the pouty, bleeding-edge design champion and he said crud to her?' Minky said.

'She would give him a blow-job in the lift.'

'If I did that to the design champion, would you provide me with an audio description?'

'Sure.'

'What are his eyes like?'

'Kind of soulful. Well, not so much soulful as desperate to be soulful.'

'Do you like him?'

There was a leaping, lucky fire in the design champion that Sid envied. The way the man tamped it all down under a surface of cool, sleepy authority, speaking in a hissy whisper so you had to lean in; Sid felt like he was being gassed. He hated him.

'I'm starting to like him,' Sid said.

'I can't tell whether you like people anymore. I can't see if you are rolling your eyes. Could we agree a sound? Like this . . .' she purred her tongue.

The lift returned, but stopped below them, between the floors, and they heard the design champion's dandelion-down voice telling someone he was stuck and agreeing that twenty minutes would be fine.

'Hi, there! We'll wait with you,' Sid called down. Don't worry.'

'I'm fine,' the design champion said. 'I'm not afraid of lifts. I'm not claustrophobic.' The phrases sounded odd, like a doll repeating pre-recorded statements.

Sid peered down into the lift car. The design champion was lying in the corner folded up like an unborn animal, his thumb in his mouth, his body quivering. Sid called out to him again and the thumb came out of this mouth and he said in a confident tone, 'I'm not afraid of lifts. I'm not claustrophobic,' then the thumb went back in again and he squeezed his eyes together tightly and rocked. The design champion stayed in that position until the engineer arrived and when the doors slid apart he was standing confident and erect with a big smile on his face, and he shook Minky's hand and asked her, in his dandelion-down voice, if she felt she had enough material for her article and she replied that she had, colours moving about in her face.

They walked down the road towards the town.

'I was thinking,' Minky said, 'that if we'd met after I'd become blind, I might not have fallen in love with you. It frightens me, Sid. I don't know what goes on in your mind.'

'Neither do I.'

'You should rip it all out and start again.'

'If it was an option, I would.'

They reached the shops. He saw a pair of sherbet-headed budgies bobbing about in a pet shop window, a dog wearing a Manchester United strip sitting in a special dog pram, a figure dressed as Bertie Bassett picking up flyers he'd spilled on the street, a tiny, old, wizened man in a baseball hat that read, I give guaranteed satisfaction. In the window of McDonald's, a woman stole a chip while her child's back was turned.

'What can you see?'

'There's a planning application tied to a lamppost. Want to know what it says?'

'Not bothered,' she said. 'I love you, Sid.'

'Palimpsest,' he said.

Coned

H E CREPT DOWN the on-slip. Typical Bank Holiday, solid from three to seven, just as the traffic girl said in her juicy, posh voice.

He should have screamed away in a cloud of dust. But how could you in this choked-up, tangled mess? Crawling off like an insect, just how Deborah would like it.

Juicy voice cooed more traffic news. Spider had rung to tell her the M55 west-bound was closed from twelve to eighteen. It was awful on the A38, horrible at a roundabout near Stoke.

It was the first time he had stormed out. Now he was trapped in a river of steel, with a thousand sea-siders, fresh from penny-falls and Whippy ice cream. He had no idea where he was going, and getting nowhere fast. According to juicy voice, the M6 had coped very well, considering the pressure.

Not Static

THERE WAS A spot of soft earth at the top of the hill overlooking the caravan site and it looked just right so I leaned the spade against a tree, unfolded the blanket I'd wrapped it in and laid it out on the grass. I looked at it for a time, lying there, precious-looking.

The hill was bleak, dusty, a place where nothing grew apart from stumpy skeletal trees. A breeze ruffled my hair, pleasant after the big-fisted heat of the caravan site. Everything felt different high up on the hill. I kneeled for a few moments, closed my eyes, said a few things in my head, then opened my eyes again, half expecting it to have gone. There it lay, still and pale. I stood and lifted the spade. Burying seemed the correct thing. It was better like this.

No one to worry us, no one to hurry us. To this dream we found. We'll gaze at the sky and try to guess what it's all about.

I placed it in the shallow hole. Shallow. Newspaper reporters make a noise about holes being shallow, as if deeper holes made everything OK, and I think I know why that is. They think it's permanent, they think it will last. But nothing lasts. Used to think everything would last. But why should it?

This can't last. This misery can't last. I must remember
that and try to control myself. Nothing lasts really. Neither
happiness nor despair. Not even life lasts very long.

It all started only a week ago. I had been paddling in the
sea with Felicity and Jamie when I noticed a faint indenta-
tion the thickness of a hair running around my upper arm. I
thought it was nothing, dismissed it, but the next day Jamie
and I were building a sand palace for Felicity's Barbie and
I was putting the finishing touches to the low wall around
the moat when Jamie said, 'Dad, what's that funny line on
your arm?'

What had been a line no thicker than a whisker was
now a shallow groove running round the whole circumference of my arm, just below the shoulder. I squeezed my
fingertips into the hollow. It was like a deep wrinkle. Maybe
that's what it was: a wrinkle. I stretched my arm to see if the
furrow would disappear. It didn't.

I continued to build the palace for Felicity's doll. The
Barbie came with a purple horse and this meant stables
and an exercise field, as well as the ten-roomed building
she had specified, so we had a lot of construction work to
do. I decided to ignore the blemish on my arm. When you
notice something odd about your body the idea becomes
all enveloping — like when I was a kid and obsessed that
my ears were monstrous flaps and slept with a heavy book
on the side of my face.

I splashed water onto the sand, scooped up a handful,
and poured it onto the palace walls to make smooth concrete whirls. Jamie and I set about moulding the runny sand
into shapely turrets and balustrades, while Felicity marked
out the horse's field.

Georgina came over with ice creams.

'Mum, has your arm got a line on it like Dad's?' Jamie said.

'I don't know, darling. I don't think so.'

'See?' Jamie poked my arm, showing the groove to Georgina.

'That's funny,' she said. 'Maybe it's how Daddy's been sleeping. Have you been leaning on something?'

I brushed sand from the wrinkle. 'I don't think so. It must have always been there.'

She, like me, pressed her fingers into the wrinkle then followed it round my arm like a needle in the groove of a record. 'Does it hurt?' she asked.

'No.'

'Has it been bleeding?'

'No.'

'Have you fallen, or cut yourself, or bumped into something?

'No.'

'It's almost like there was something tied around your arm and then it's been taken away and left a wound. But you say it doesn't hurt?'

'No. It's not sore. But I think I'll put my shirt back on—this sun is scorching.'

On the way back, we passed Hooch sitting outside her caravan scratching numbers into her ledger. Hooch was the odd job woman and had the caravan next to ours. She looked after everything—changing gas bottles, fitting light bulbs, unblocking drains, and organising engineers for the more technical problems. She was a skinny, unclean woman with long straight black hair, a severe fringe and lipstick of a dark red colour, which made her teeth glow margarine yellow. But you seldom saw them because she never, ever smiled. She had few callers and there wasn't a man. The solitary nature of her job seemed to give her pleasure. In the evening she sat outside her caravan filling in a ledger. We knew what she was writing about because we heard her talking about it on her mobile phone: the flickering light in number 46, the leaky shower tray in number 49, the smell of gas in number 94.

Hooch had slung a hammock between her caravan and an adjacent tree and when she'd finished writing in her ledger, she clambered into it to read her book. Always a biography, and always of a sporting figure. We used to sit outside our caravan a few yards away from her, drinking cheap wine and looking at the stars. She was a restful presence and some kind of companionable relationship between us developed, which was hard to describe. When she wasn't there we felt somehow incomplete.

Hooch listened to one CD over and over again — an album of Noel Coward songs, louche, loungey tunes from another era, with desperate, yearning, lonely words. A soft piano tinkled over a ukulele rhythm:

> *Speak low, Johnny,*
> *Tip toe, Johnny,*
> *Go slow, Johnny,*
> *Go slow.*

'Hiya Hooch,' I called out. She lifted her head from Tennis Ace, the story of Chris Evett, and pointed her ferocious little eyes at me. Her hair looked greasy and held the tracks of her comb.

'Hummph,' said Hooch.

'Hooch, our fridge door won't close properly and I was wondering whether . . .'

Hooch held up her hand to stop me, then reached under the table from where she produced a polythene bag with a plastic device inside. 'Use this to click around the door,' she said. 'I knew about that problem.'

'So you had that ready for us?'

'Yes,' said Hooch.

'In case we asked?'

'Yes.'

'But what if we had just struggled on and didn't ask?'

'It's up to you,' she said. 'I don't interfere, I just help when I am asked.'

I looked at her for a moment. There were times when she seemed half buried in some sediment of despair.

'But you knew about — oh. never mind,' I said. 'Enjoy your book, Hooch.'

From her stereo Noel Coward cooed that all he needed was: *A room with a view and you and no one to give advice.*

When I woke up the next morning, the first thing I did was feel my arm. I sat upright in shock. It was definitely worse than yesterday. My finger went in deep, up to the first knuckle. I lifted it to see whether it there was any effect on my movements, but there didn't seem to be.

I made a cup of tea and sat on the step of the caravan. Six-thirty. People were assembling for that day's trip. A melon farm? Or was it a pearl factory? I lifted the arm above my head. No problem. I went over to the terrace table and tried to lift the parasol holder which was anchored by a heavy container of water. I could just about shift it, the strength in my arm didn't seem to be affected. While holding the parasol aloft, I caught a glimpse of Hooch at her window, washing a glass at the sink. She was looking at me and frowning more than usual. If it wasn't for her thick fringe I imagined I would have seen deep furrows in her brow like dark canals.

When Georgina appeared I told her I was worried. 'The situation with my arm,' I called it and she laughed.

'The situation,' she said back at me.

I told her that I definitely hadn't had it since I was a kid, that it was something new. Again she asked about pain, and infection, and cuts and accidents, and again I told her no.

'Well,' she said, 'I think it's nothing to worry about, but maybe you should go to the campsite health centre and see what they say.'

I stopped at Hooch's hammock. Her bare feet were hanging over the end. Hairs grew from her big toes.

'Do you know anything about the campsite doctor, Hooch?'

She looked up and swept her eyes from my heels to my scalp, instantly bored by the query.

'What's up, like? You got a cold or summat?'

I smiled. 'I need to see the local sawbones. You're not in charge of our physical health as well as our gas bottles, are you, Hooch?'

Her expression didn't change. 'No,' she said. 'Just repairs to the caravans, like.'

'I know,' I said.

Her face under the stiff line of her fringe showed no flicker of emotion. 'People think they're funny, like,' she said. 'Dead funny. You know what? Nobody's funny nowadays, that's the truth. You need a doctor, like? Uh?'

'I could do with seeing one today.'

From her stereo Noel Coward pleaded:

Please be kind.
When you're lonely-if you're lonely
Call me-call me-anyhow.
If you want me-need me-love me
Tell me,
Tell me,
Tell me now!

'The doctor's surgery is from nine till eleven, thereabouts.' Hooch said. 'He'll see you and he'll give it to you straight. But you have to have your green slip.'

'Oh, I've got the green slip.'

I thought I saw the flicker of a smile before her face resumed its default position of an aggrieved grimace.

Now I was kneeling next to the hole. Now I was getting rid of it. Getting rid of things. I felt much better. It had felt for a time back then as if someone, somewhere, was disassembling me, disaggregating me, taking me apart, fleck by bitter fleck, as if they wanted to shatter me into a thousand spores, toss me out of the window into a shrieking storm. It was as if they needed a cutting from me to stick in the ground, a whole new me to spurt out, to break me up, seed me all over, in every fold of earth, every pleat of skin, in Hooch's greasy hair, in the angry heat of some dead dog yard. To put me in places where people don't go, places they've forgotten, places they never knew they came from that they go back to in the end.

One more look, one more touch, before the dirt. I had to hide it. Cover it. Cover it with dirt. We call it dirt, but is it dirty? What is on dirt that is dirty? Can dirt be cleaned? Can something be taken way from dirt to make it clean again and if so, what would be left? Am I what is left when dirt is taken from dirt?

I wondered about leaving the lid off. But it looked so fragile, so needful, yearning for its blanket of dust. Happy under soil. Safe and warm and tired. I wished I could join it. Maybe that's what it wanted.

As happy and contented as birds upon a tree.
High above the mountains and the sea.

I touched it again. One last time. Like placing my hand on the skin of a some mummified saint. It felt warm, which was impossible, and soft too. Was that a pulse? A trembling, a tingle? Was there a tiny blush of pink in the fingertips?

I began to scrape the dirt over the top.

They'll come a time in the future when I shan't mind about
this anymore.

Later that night we had gone to the campsite bar. It was kids' karaoke and Jamie wanted to do Eminem and we'd said he could as long as he did the radio edit with the gaps for the swearing.

Earlier, in the shower, I had a really good look at my arm. There was a groove all the way round, a definite groove. It seemed even deeper than before at the beach. I could insert the tip of my thumb right inside and trail it round the whole circumference.

'Ladies and gentlemen, Jamie Crowther.'

Little Jamie, hair gelled-up, hollered the words to 'Stan' while the Dido track warbled away and we watched, utterly rapt. Georgina gripped my knee. 'Look at him. I can't believe he's ours.'

'I know,' I said, and squeezed her hand, grinning like an idiot.

The doctor was a young Spanish man with excellent English who listened carefully and nodded seriously as I described the opening that had appeared from nowhere on my arm.

'Have you been OK otherwise?'

'Fit as a fiddle,' I said.

'OK, let's have a look.' He moved me over to the examination couch. I sat on the edge and removed my shirt and the doctor looked at the strange aperture, inserting his fingers just as I had and checking to see how far round it went. 'Just move your arm a little for me,' he murmured, and I worked my shoulder up and down. The split opened and closed like the sucking lips of a horrible shellfish.

'You can put your shirt back on,' he said. 'And sit back down over there.' I did as he asked and he looked at me and tapped his pen on his pad of paper. 'You say it appeared yesterday?' he asked.

'Yes.'

'Well, it looks to me like it's always been there. It looks like it's healed perfectly, but that at one time it was some kind of wound. Maybe from tying something tightly around it. Have you had anything tied tightly around it? Some sort of ligature?'

'No.'

'Can you use your arm? Can you lift and stretch?'

'It feels fine.'

'Do you use any drugs. Anything like that?'

'Not really.' The fact was I smoked spliffs most

weeks — most days if I was honest — but I didn't see how that was relevant. 'The odd glass of wine.' Bottle more like.

He looked to the side for a beat. 'Any mental health problems — depression, anxiety?'

'No more than any one else. We all get down from time to time.'

'That's true. Well,' he said putting down his pen, 'if you can use the arm and you're in no pain and there's no sign of infection, I don't think there's much we can do. Just keep an eye on it and come back if it gets any worse.'

Georgina and Jamie and Felicity were waiting for me when I got back. I had promised that we would drive in to the local town where there was a market and fairground rides.

'Everything OK?' Said Georgina, flapping her arm like a chicken.

'He said to keep an eye on it.'

'Let's do that then.'

As we packed up the car, I saw Hooch looking at us out of her caravan window as she watered a plant. She raised her eyebrows in a peculiar way.

I wandered around the market, making a conscious effort not to check my arm. My hand wandered up there once or twice, but I corrected it. The problem would seem worse if I kept checking all the time. I vowed to leave it alone for a whole day then check in the morning.

The market was crawling with tourists in combat shorts and lumpy off-road sandals. I could never see the attraction of markets. We have markets at home and they are colourful and exciting too, but we never go to them. The stalls were stocked with oddly-shaped cheeses, glossy vegetables, olives and big, ugly, dried fish. Jamie and Felicity liked a stall that sold dogs, rats and chickens, and we spent a long time hanging about there. After a few hours I had completely forgotten about the situation with my arm. Jamie bought a miniature kite and Felicity a wooden parrot that flapped its wings when you pulled a lever.

When we got back to the car she gave me it and I yanked on the lever. 'Squawk, squawk, hello Felicity, where's Jamie?' I said. But operating the toy parrot made me aware that the arm felt quite a bit different now than it had the day before. It felt much longer than the other arm, like it was heavier. I returned the parrot to Felicity and went behind the car where I pretended to check something in the boot. I lifted up my shirt sleeve. When I saw what had happened I said, 'Oh!' as if I had been struck. I trembled. I felt faint. The opening had grown much larger, to such an extent that it wasn't a wrinkle or an opening any more. It was as if a huge chunk of flesh had been gouged out of my upper arm, as though it had been turned on a lathe the way you make the indents in table legs. The space was now the width of three fingers and the piece connecting my arm to my shoulder the thickness of a broom handle.

'Georgina, come here a minute.' She got out of the passenger seat and came over to where I was sitting on the lip of the car boot. 'Look at it now,' I gazed up at her imploringly. I must have looked like a sick puppy.

She looked at the arm and I saw panic flash across her face. But then she calmed herself. 'Is it hurting?' she said.

'No.'

'And you can still use it?

'Yes. Look.' I lifted the arm and touched her hair. I sensed her flinch a little as if she was afraid, as if my arm was some kind of monster.

'What's wrong?' I smiled at her. 'I don't think you can catch it.' For the first time, Georgina looked worried, and for some reason, this made me feel a little better, as if I had passed some of my fear on to her.

'Maybe you should, sort of, have it up in a sling? Maybe you should rest it and then the flesh will, I don't know, grow back?' She looked at me for a long time. 'Oh, Roger,' she said finally. 'What have you been doing?'

'Doing?' I said. 'What could I have been doing that would cause this?'

'Mum,' said Felicity from the back seat. 'Can we go back now. It's little Mr and Mrs Universe tonight and me and Jamie have entered. Come on.'

'Will you be able to drive?' Georgina asked me.

'Yes,' I said. 'It feels fine. Just the idea is a bit weird, that's all.'

Everything bad safely hidden away under the earth. I patted the dirt down, stamped it flat with my boots, then looked about me for some kind of marker — stones, or a stick for a cross. But why? A lump of meat. We talk of minds, of souls, but it's just a ball of nerves. Fingers remembering movements, a pattern of piano keys, or a lover's curves, or changing gear in a car, or throwing a cricket ball. Recalling electronic pulses.

The breeze strummed the telegraph wires, a low hum, making the wires sing. But do we bury these wires? Do we dress in dark suits and shiny shoes to accompany them to the scrap yard, do we sing when they are dismantled, do we cry when the poles are burned or shudder when the connectors are melted for tin? No. We do things, we stop doing them. End of. Nothing has ever really happened if you don't tell anyone about it and no one writes it down.

I found a rusted coke can and tore it open. Its shiny, inner skin. Twisted it into an antic shape, distressed and hopeful at the same time, twin aluminium arms curling up towards the starless sky. I placed it on the spot. Despite the marker, I knew no one would find it. But I'll know where it is; I'll know what I did, and what I did will always be with me.

That sounds a paradise few could fail to choose.
With fingers entwined we'll find relief from the preachers

I set off down the hill to the campsite. The lights from the caravans below glowed soft-yellow. Seagulls called — wild, haunting — and music boomed from the club house. A plane took off from the airport on the other side of the island, a steep trajectory over the mountains and out towards the sea, tilting silently like an owl, its lights winking in the dusk.

But I can look back and say quite peacefully and cheer-
fully how silly I was. No, no I don't want that time to come
hither.

Hooch was sitting outside, talking into her mobile when we got back, her ledger open in front of her. She stopped talking and switched off the phone as we walked past and looked at us with no expression.

'The fridge is fine with that clip holding it shut.' Georgina said to her. 'Thank you.'

'That's what it's for,' said Hooch.

Georgina stopped at her table and said. 'Do you ever miss home, Hooch? It must be a long season.'

'Five and a half months. It's what I do. It's very cold at home. Scotland is very cold. I like to be outside, like.'

'Did you do the same sort of work in Scotland?'

'No.'

'What did you used to do?'

'I was a social worker.'

Georgina nodded and followed the rest of us into our caravan. 'She's a miserable bitch,' she whispered to me.

'What's a social worker?' said Felicity.

'It's like a life coach for poor people,' I said.

We heard her turn her CD player on, Coward's words drifting over again, as if she were using the songs to communicate something to us:

> *And when you're so blue,*
> *Wet through*
> *And thoroughly woe-begone,*
> *Why must the show go on?*

I was carrying a tray of drinks back from the bar when I noticed that the arm with the situation was hanging down much longer than the other one. We sat in silence and watched the Mr and Miss Universe competition. Jamie had dressed himself up as Tarzan, Felicity was a fairy, and after the competition they danced on the stage to the latest summer disco hits which involved regimented dance routines known by every kid. Georgina and I watched the gyrating children and hummed along to the cheesey pop. We drank a carafe of cheap red wine and I said I wanted some more and she said, yes, so we drank more. If I were honest I wanted to be drunk so I would be sure to get to sleep. I didn't want to lie there worrying about my arm.

Hooch was outside in her hammock, drinking a glass of something amber coloured and reading the life of George Best by the light of the caravan. She was smoking a cigarette. Coward sang out from the machine:

Go slow, Johnny,
Maybe she'll come to her senses
If you'll give her a chance.
People's feelings are sensitive plants

I mumbled, 'Evening, Hooch,' and a grunt came back.

Inside the caravan I wrapped a towel around the affected area and went to bed. I had a vague idea that the newly-exposed flesh might need protecting, or that maybe the warmth would encourage it to grow back. I fell asleep and dreamt of diseased bodies and hideous limbless creatures.

The next day I sat up in bed and immediately unwrapped the towel. My arm flopped out and dangled down. It seemed to hang much lower than it had yesterday. I looked at my shoulder and saw that it was now attached by only a sliver of flesh, no thicker than a pencil. I was afraid to let this fragile-looking thread take the weight, so I held the arm with my other arm and went and sat on the step of the caravan, nursing it like a baby. Fear came down like a cage. I wished I was at home. My own doctor, Dr Brazenose, would know what to do. These foreign doctors, maybe they weren't so up to date. Or maybe it was some sort of Spanish condition. The doctor didn't seem so surprised about it, after all.

I looked over at the dark windows of Hooch's caravan. I could hear the faint murmur of her radio. When it wasn't Noel Coward, she listened to the World Service — fat plummy voices growling on and on about foreign uprisings, dysfunctional economies and obscure election results in former Soviet states. I heard Jamie and Felicity scuffling about and Jamie skipped over and jumped on my back. 'Careful of my sore arm, darling,' I said.

'Let's have a look. Have you still got a hole in it?'

'No, it's OK,' I said. I didn't want him to see it like that.

'What time are we going to the water park?' he asked.

'When Mum gets up. I'll go and see if she's awake.'

In the bedroom, I shook Georgina. 'Georgina, look at it now,' I said. 'Look.' I let the arm dangle down. I could still move it, although it did take a bit more effort, but it was now a good six inches longer than it should be.

She sat up and reached for her spectacles. When she put them on she gasped. 'Oh my God, Roger, what did you do?'

'I didn't do anything.'

'What did you do?' she repeated. We both stared at the arm for a long time. Then she said, 'Come here,' and she hugged me. 'Don't worry. We'll take you to the town. There's a hospital there. A big one. They'll know what to do.'

'What if . . .' I said.

'Don't be stupid,' she said. 'That's not going to happen, have you ever heard of that happening to anyone?'

I got into the shower and gave myself a really good wash ahead of the hospital visit. I was using the affected arm to wash under my other arm when the situation got much, much worse. There was a kind of twang at my shoulder and the arm fell away, the upper part hitting the shower floor, the hand falling to rest against my thigh. 'Shit!' I cried. 'Fuck, oh no!' I looked at the shoulder expecting to see blood. But there was nothing. I stood with the shower gushing and steam gathering around me. I bent and gripped the arm by its hand. Then I rested it on the floor and with my good hand examined the place from where it had fallen. It was completely smooth, as if the arm had never been there. I bent down and felt the severed end of the detached arm too and it was smooth as well.

I turned off the shower. How was I going to explain this to Georgina and the kids? Waves of guilt and despair swept through me.

I wrapped the arm up in a towel and set off across the site to the main gates. I walked and walked, holding the arm close to my chest, tears burning my cheeks. I walked for about an hour, but eventually the heat got too much and I collapsed on to a bench. I unwrapped the arm and looked at it. It didn't look any paler then the rest of my body. I touched it. It didn't feel cold, like a dead thing; it felt the same as before. I interlocked the fingers of my good hand with the fingers of my severed arm and sat there. Cars swished by on their way to the beach. I closed my eyes against the scorching sun.

Sometime later there was an angry crump of gravel followed by Georgina's voice, sounding tight and clenched. 'Roger! We've been looking for you everywhere.'

I climbed into the car sheepishly. 'It's my arm,' I said. Georgina looked at the swaddled bundle then the stump at my shoulder. 'Oh Roger, grow up. Are you ill?'

'Well, no,'

'Well if you're not ill you're just going to have to get on with it, aren't you? Sometimes your self-indulgence is so pathetic. Don't ruin everyone's holiday over this.'

Felicity and Jamie were quiet all the way back. But I heard Jamie say quietly to Felicity, 'Dad's arms fell off,' and I heard Felicity giggle.

Hooch was standing outside our caravan when we got back.

'You've got a blockage,' she said, accusingly.

'Oh?' said Georgina.

'It's affecting the others on the row, so I will have to fix it, like. Do you mind if I turn you off for half an hour?'

'Well, I was just about to cook,' Georgina said.

Hooch stared at her, unsmiling. 'I'm doing my job.' she said.

Hooch fixed the blockage, then lay down in her hammock to read, with her CD player leaking out Coward's usual sentimental drivel:

> *Till you know that you know*
> *Your stars are bright for you,*
> *Right for you*

We didn't go down the bar that night. Jamie and Felicity went to the playground on their own. They were upset to see the arm, so I agreed to keep it wrapped up while they were around. But I kept it nearby so I could see where it was. We sat outside and drank wine and looked at the stars. You could see Venus. Mercury, too. When it became time to go to bed, I unwrapped the arm, pulled back the covers and lay it on the sheet on my side of the bed. Georgina looked at it in horror. 'What are you doing?'

'I'm going to bed,' I said.

'With that?' she said.

'But it's me. It's my arm'. I didn't want to be parted from the limb. I had a vague notion that during the night it might rejoin my body in the same way it had strangely become detached. I got in next to it and cuddled it close. A cold, clammy hot-water bottle.

'If you are sleeping with that arm, then I am sleeping on the sofa.'

'Fine,' I said, and rolled over.

The next evening, Georgina said told me that she was going to stay with Hooch for a few nights. 'This, you know, this arm thing, it's a bit, eeeuch You know how I am with snails and things like that.'

'Hooch?'

'Just till the end of the holiday.'

'I can't imagine you staying with Hooch.'

'You can't imagine me? You don't imagine me, I'm just there.'

We looked at each other for a few moments in silence.

'Snails?' I said.

My face burned with shame and anger as I watched her drag her suitcase through the gravel to Hooch's caravan. Hooch was at the table doing her ledger and she didn't even look up as Georgina lifted the case up the step and into her home.

Georgina stayed with Hooch for the last three days of the holiday. We were about to set off for the airport when Georgina discovered I had packed the arm into my carry-on luggage.

'Roger, I cant believe you still have that. You can't take it home with us.'

'Well, I'm not leaving it here. What would I do? Chuck it in a skip?'

'You know what they said at the hospital. They couldn't reattach it. The nerves were all dead, like it had never been attached. You're so sentimental, Roger. It's an arm, that's all. The human spirit is not present in that piece of flesh. There's nothing of you, the man I love, in that arm.'

But I was adamant. 'The arm comes with me.' I said. 'I don't care what anyone says.'

At the airport it showed up on the X-ray and they took me into a special room. The police became involved. It took a long time, but eventually they were made to understand that there was no crime involved. But they wouldn't let me take it on the plane. They spent some time deciding on its classification. It wasn't a dead body, so what was it? They eventually decided it was meat.

'My arm is not raw meat,' I said.

After some discussion they let me take the arm away with a promise to return the next day with the right paperwork, and Georgina stalked off to the boarding gate without looking back, pulling behind her Felicity and Jamie, who twisted their necks to stare at me, eyes wet, faces red, lips trembling.

Hooch was standing outside her caravan with a suitcase. She was waiting for a taxi to the airport. She told me, in blurting breathless sentences, all about Georgina and her. I pushed her inside the caravan, and from that point everything went badly.

But now it was all going to be all right. I stopped on the hill and looked down at Hooch's home. Empty. People come and people go, then disappear. That's about it really, that's all you can say. I took a swig of water, felt giddy like the first touches of flu.

Hooch's caravan smelt still of Georgina. I made tea and went outside and sat in the hammock. I picked up Hooch's mobile and listened to the messages. The light in number 46 was flickering, the shower tray in number 49 was leaking, there was a smell of gas in number 94. I would attend to these problems the next day. I picked up Hooch's book. A page was folded over a third of the way in. Two-thirds of a story she would never hear.

I looked over the site to the mountains. I could see an eagle high in the sky, slowly circling at its great height. I wondered if it could see me.

A room with a view and you and no one to give advice.
That sounds a paradise few could fail to choose.

I thought of Georgina and Felicity and Jamie. One day I would go to the beach again and build another sand palace. It would help me remember that once there was more than just us. Still, I am better off here, in the sun. Nothing ever seems so bad when the sun is shining. I looked over to the box where my arm lay. Later I would take it out, sit with it in my lap again, as I did most nights. Otherwise I would forget. It would forget.

I want to remember every minute, always, always to the end of my days.

People had moved in to the next-door caravan, our old caravan. They kept chatting to me, trying to get me to go out with them, down to the bar, to be sociable. To share. They once asked me what I was holding, what was in the bundle, what was so precious. Was it a baby, they joked. They were worried about me. I ignored them. I like to be alone. I clicked on Hooch's CD player.

We'll bill and we'll coo and sorrow will never come,
Or will it ever come
Always torn, always thinking what if,
of possibilities, of the way things could have been
if only
I'll see you somewhere
I'll see you sometime
Darling

HALF CLOSED

The Only Man with Fire

THE DOOR WENT and it was Hilary McNally, the woman from the opposite bank who put in the objection to his extension. She hated the idea of floor-to-ceiling glass walls, despite him explaining how the interior and the river would meld seamlessly together. He assumed she wished to expand further on why his abomination of a building was an affront to the vernacular style of Denshaw, when he noticed that she was smiling and saying something about a hospice-to-hospice walk.

'I don't do sponsoring stuff,' he said.

'No, no, we're not asking you to take part,' she said, her smile fading. 'It's just that for new residents there's a tradition. We ask them to light the missile cake at the hospice-to-hospice after-walk party.'

Simon made his face look puzzled and friendly at the same time.

'It's a collection of fireworks,' Hilary explained. 'Tied together for displays.' She handed him a box. Liberator Missile Cake it said in florescent writing against tongues of fire and plumes of smoke.

He looked over to his extension, covered with tarpaulin because of Ms McNally's objections. Lighting a few fireworks couldn't hurt.

'It's at the post office green,' she said. 'Six o'clock.'

On his way to the post office green, Simon realised that there was a problem with his offer to help. He was a non-smoker and had no matches or lighter and didn't want to embarrass himself by having to asking for help.

Then, outside the Oddfellows, he saw a man standing on his own, smoking. This man stood outside the Oddfellows every single night and never seemed to go inside, whatever the weather.

Simon introduced himself and the man stuck out his hand. 'Tom Sutherland,' he said. He was large, dressed all in denim, with a wild bushy beard dotted with tobacco and ash. He listened to Simon's request carefully, checking a few points of factual accuracy to make sure he understood the request.

'So,' Tom Sutherland said after a long pause, 'you need fire. The people of Denshaw need fire, so they need Tom Sutherland. They didn't need Tom Sutherland's fire on the Community Woods Committee. They didn't need Tom Sutherland's fire in the Operatic Society. They didn't need Tom Sutherland's fire on the hospice-to-hospice walk.'

'Oh, it is for the hospice-to-hospice walk,' Simon said.

Tom Sutherland turned on him abruptly. 'I meant the actual walk. The six and a half kilometres. Not the after-walk party.'

Simon was wondering why there were two hospices so close together, but didn't voice this thought.

'You can have my fire,' Tom said. 'If I can light the missile cake myself.'

'I don't know,' said Simon, 'it's organised by Hilary McNally.'

'McNally.' Tom Sutherland hawked a frothy globule of saliva up from his throat and shot it over Simon's shoulder and into the road. 'I light the missile cake,' he said, quietly, 'or there's no fire. That's what's going to happen.'

Everyone stopped talking when Simon approached with Tom Sutherland. Tom grinned at the crowd but no one said hello or nodded. Hilary lifted her hands to her head.

Tom Sutherland lit the missile cake. Coloured flames and balls of fire shot up, but there were no whoops or aaahs from anybody apart from Tom Sutherland who made a few oooh noises, which he managed to make sound sinister. When the fireworks stopped, the participants of the hospice-to-hospice walk stood in silence looking at their feet. Then Tom Sutherland began to sing. It was a strange, toneless, lilting tune made up of gibberish words and each line ended in the word 'hey'. As his singing grew louder, he began to dance a frenzied jig, his big motorbike boots flying up and down in the air, and he continued to do this for several minutes until everyone drifted off and left him whirling and stomping in the light of the bonfire.

Simon cleared up the fragments of ash from the missile cake. He didn't want the blame for spoiling the post office green. Tom Sutherland was still singing and hopping up and down when Simon set off up the hill to begin removing the tarpaulin from his extension before ringing his builder.

People Who Don't Belong

S WISHING MEANS SWAPPING designer clothes, but William the newsagent didn't understand the word 'designer', so his George of Asda sports tops went into the pile along with Culcheth's best suits, frocks and shoes. Just because you've run the newsagent's for 20 years doesn't mean you fit in.

As predicted, William's sports tops were the only items left at the end, and Marion was wondering what to do when a young man wandered into the parish hall, swinging a see-through Risley carrier bag; standard issue for an ex-inmate's few possessions.

Marion greeted him with a big wraparound smile as her cupped hand moved towards his elbow ready to escort him to the door, but he explained that he was here for the clothes swapping, and opened his Risley bag to reveal an elegant Prada top. It had been his lucky shirt, he explained, worn hopefully to his hearing. Now it had dark connotations.

Marion looked out of the window to where the concrete prison walls stretched along the road.

The man wanted to swap the Prada top for as many

cheap, basic shirts as was possible, and he wondered if this was allowed under the rules of swishing.

It was, and Marion shoved all of William the newsagent's Asda tops into a Harvey Nicks carrier and handed it to the ex-prisoner. Then she passed the Prada shirt to William who screwed up his eyes at it before pulling it on over his jumper. He sat looking at Marion and the ex-prisoner with a big smile on his face. Marion knew what William would be thinking. He would be thinking that this Prada shirt would help him fit in. After 20 years, a shirt was all he needed. He didn't realise it wasn't about his taste, or even his class. It was William himself they disliked, with his smell of wet newspapers and juicy fruit chewing gum. The way he brushed the pavement in front of his shop, whistling Carpenters' songs and doing an annoying dance-like movement with his shoulders. The way he hadn't replied to any of Marion's texts for three and a half months.

So Much Noise

DONALD HAD BEEN seeing Julia for fourteen weeks, so it seemed only right that he should invite her to his place in the country. But it wasn't as it sounded. A rough-cast two-up-two-down the colour of porridge in a terrace of pit cottages that, owing to subsidence, bulged out in the middle like squat men with beer bellies. A post office stood at one end, a pub at the other, and nothing else for eleven and a half miles. Across the valley you could make out a similar row of dwellings, a dim grey smudge against the bracken. Donald's row was called Lamplugh, the grey smudge, Arlecdon.

With no car to explore the area, there wasn't much to do, so each day Donald placed wooden stools on the pavement and they sat there, staring at the mountains. The mountains had names. One was called Scarsdale, one Red Pike, another Striding Edge. Rising up behind was Green Gable.

'Look,' Donald would say. 'A buzzard,' and Julia craned her head to see a dark angular silhouette like that of a pumped-up pigeon. He went on like this, and she watched his mouth as it formed the words, the sounds becoming gibberish. She hadn't realised he was knowledgeable about the countryside. She'd never been interested in scenery. Scenery was what happened in the background and Julia was a foreground person. She realised then that Donald might not be her exact type. She'd met him a week after Jigger left, at a time when her life had felt a little unmoored, and if she were honest, Donald was an aisle-end decision.

They had to sit on the pavement because Donald had sold the back garden to his neighbour, Oliver, who needed extra space for his llamas. The lamas would press their slimy noses against the kitchen window and stare in with sad, imploring eyes. They had no reason to be sad, because they weren't about to be killed or eaten; they were for wool. Possibly they missed Peru. Yet why, Julia couldn't guess, because they were all born here, Donald told her, in Lamplugh, in West Cumbria, in the North of England.

So here she was, in the Lake District. Yet it wasn't the Lake District, not really. The house was just outside the National Park, which was why the properties were cheap enough for Donald, a year-one teaching assistant. It was a good place to be. Lake District views without scone and ice cream tourism slammed in your face. You could get to the lakes within five minutes in any direction. If you had a car, that is, which they didn't. So they enjoyed the view. The fact that they were away from the city, away from things to do like cinemas and theatres and restaurants and café-bars and gigs and all their friends and family and satellite TV with Sopranos repeats, was not a problem. Never mind. Bye, bye city. They had Scarsdale, and Red Pike and Green Gable rising up behind, and maybe later the buzzard would fly past again.

Each day they enjoyed the view until boredom dumped them in the pub with the farmers, turnip-faced men with blurry voices who talked of agricultural subsidies and quad bikes, or played the quiz machine with its spinning ribbons of light and churning, moaning noises, which in the end sent Julia and Donald out into the beer garden to look again at the mountains or at the grey smudge of Arlecdon where Julia imagined another glum couple staring back at them across acres of bracken.

Nothing to do, nothing to see, no one to talk to, nowhere to go. Many times Julia couldn't think of anything to say and a weighted silence fell about them, broken only by an RAF jet roaring past, hugging the contours of the valley, the delayed explosive rush of its engine making Julia jump out of her skin every time.

On their way back from the pub Donald stopped. 'Watch this.' He cupped his hands over his mouth and made a hooting noise, which echoed across the valley. Julia went to speak. 'Shush, listen.'

Julia heard it. A similar sound, but slightly different in pattern, tone, and inflection. An owl. An owl was returning his call.

'I learned it from a book about bird watching. It's a mating call. The owl thinks I'm a female in season. It will come over here soon, swooping about, hunting, for the female. For me.'

Julia laughed with the particular edge of disdain she reserved for Donald's sparks of trainspotter-like wisdom. 'Do you think,' she said, 'it will break in to the house and take you roughly from behind while you sleep? You should watch out, teasing like that. They will say you were asking for it. Seriously, how big are these owls?'

'They're small little tiny things,' Donald cupped an imaginary one between his palms. 'I'll show you a picture when we get back. You're thinking about eagle owls. They're the biggest, and have been known to carry off small babies.'

'That's what they always say. You wonder, don't you? Like that dingo thing. It's the way country people reduce the numbers of their children.'

In bed, Julia became highly charged with desire for Donald and, weirdly, it was connected to her thinking about the little round owl, fired up with lust, diving up and down in the sky, searching for its mate, testosterone screaming about in its trembling little body. She thought of Donald being raped by an owl and wondered whether there were occult porn sites dedicated to that sort of thing. She's heard about sex with animals, but with birds? This was ultra-sick, a perversion too far. She was sorry she'd thought about it. But she couldn't stop her mind turning the idea over and over. Did owls have penises? What were the mechanics of bird sex? She had some vague notions about fish — that the male spurted its sperm into the water while the female did the same with its eggs; possibly birds did this in the air. But bird's eggs and sperm would rain down all the while, especially in cities, with all those pigeons and sparrows and starlings

Donald fell asleep abruptly as usual, and snored softly.

The cloying dark. The suffocating emptiness. Julia's heart pattered in her chest and blood hammered in her veins. She felt tiny and alone. The silence was solid, predatory, and seemed to have its own sound, a pulsing hiss that pressed in on her from all sides; she longed to be back in the city where warm folds of hum and clatter nursed her to sleep.

The next night there was a darts match at the pub and Donald was obliged to take part, so Julia sat outside with a book. There wasn't another soul about so she cupped her hands and tried out the owl sound. It worked — the other owl returned her call. It was exciting, communicating with the animal kingdom and she did it again. The sound seemed to come from near to Arlecdon, the grey smudge of a village opposite and, as it would be ages before Donald finished his game of darts, she picked up the Maglight and set off down the footpath to Arlecdon, hooting happily as she went. She would locate her feathery paramour and take a picture of it with her mobile. How impressed Donald would be.

As she walked, the hoots of the other owl grew closer and closer. However, the owl didn't seem to be seeking her out. She expected it to fly over, but it didn't. Everything became so very dark. She flicked off her torch to test the depth of the blackness. It was unutterable. No moon, no stars, like a cave. No glow from the pub, no lights from Arlecdon. A cow lowed nearby, a dog barked in the distance and she panicked, flicked on the torch and followed the path again, this time with a new urgency in her step. Soon she reached Arlecdon and could hear the hooting coming from behind the row of houses. She rounded the corner and there he was. A man in a woollen hat and clumpy, layered clothes sitting on a bench under the sole street lamp in the whole of West Cumbria. A skinny dog was by his side. The man was facing across the valley towards Lamplugh. He lifted his hand to his mouth and made the owl sound. She went closer, preparing a half-amused, half-amazed expression for her face, ready to introduce herself as the owl from across the valley, when the man bowed his head and rested it in his hands. He made some more noises, but they weren't those of an owl. Half of his fist was in his mouth and he was sobbing wretchedly, his shoulders quivering, each sniffling intake of breath making a reedy squeaking sound that seemed alarmingly loud in the dark. Puffs of air rose up from him in little clouds.

She stayed where she was, in the shadows. The dog didn't lick his hand or snuggle up like a pet in a film.

It was their last morning and they were waiting outside the front of the house for the taxi to Whitehaven when a jet plane screeched towards them following a different path to usual, zooming overhead at such low altitude you felt that you could jump up and touch it. The pilot's face in the cockpit was an orangey blur. Donald explained that if you were high on a mountain, the jets sometimes flew below you, gliding by silently, the engine's thunder following seconds later when the plane was well out of sight.

Sure enough, the plane was long gone when they heard its visceral crashing boom. It was followed by a different sound: Oliver next door shouting for Donald to come and help. Round the back they found one of the llamas on its side and Oliver bent over it, thumping its chest with his fist.

'I knew it,' Oliver said. 'Call the vet for me, would you, Don. Those fucking jets. I was stood at the sink washing up, and I heard it go over and I saw him trembling like he'd been electrocuted, then he tossed his head back and collapsed.'

Donald cancelled their taxi and they waited with Oliver for the vet. Oliver was inconsolable and wouldn't leave the llama's side. He explained over and over how he would sue those bastards at the RAF, sue them within an inch. Though she didn't voice her doubts, Julia wondered how he would prove it. Two things happening at the same time doesn't mean they are linked, not in a legal sense. Although she herself was convinced the plane had killed the Llama, Oliver's analysis struck her as simple, rural.

The vet took the llama away, Donald made tea, and the three of them sat outside and looked at the mountains. Oliver explained Llamas weren't used to sudden loud noises. The mountains of Peru were peaceful—wind, birds, shepherd's whistling. What was it with people? Why did they have to make so much noise?

The Half-Life of Songs

THE VILLAGERS WERE waiting for us in The Dog. 'Bernice, Alan!' they called out with breathless excitement.

Nora, a delicate, bony woman with tiny hooves for feet, stepped forward. 'So nice to see you both. Reg at the post office told us your names. This is Miles. The landlord. He is looking forward to Mr Coulthard becoming one of The Dog barflies. But first of all, about your bijou house warming the other night, next time you host a social gathering at Glebe cottage, don't forget to give Miles a little notice. He has his events to plan.'

I looked at Nora's shiny gold slippers, her ochre, wrinkly skin like an overdone chicken.

'Events?'

'Quiz nights, hot pot suppers, sometimes a modern comedian. It all happens here. Imagine: karaoke booked, but all the villagers chez Coulthard chomping down on Bernice's exquisite vol-au-vents. No one in the boozer, and 'I Will Survive' belting into an empty room. This place, Bernice,' she pressed Bernice's arm, as if testing for ripeness, discovering her environment the way beasts do, 'is the hub of it all.'

Drinks in hand, we set off towards an alcove, but Nora leapt in front of us. 'You can't go off on your own like that,

Bernice and Alan.' She looked as if she was about to faint. 'No, no, no. Mr Coulthard must stand with the men.' She nodded to a herd of check and gabardine figures, laughing conspiratorially. 'And you, my dear, will sit with us girls. Come.'

A man from a farm told me about a brand of sheep-dip that glowed in the dark, about the use of tax-free red diesel, and about the ram with one testicle who was the best inseminator in the valley. Then he clapped his broad hands together and called out, 'Way, hay, hay, karaoke!'

Nora handed out the song list, explaining that the people who had Glebe cottage before us did 'Avenues and Alley-ways' and 'Stand By Your Man'. What would our songs be? They'd heard we were modern.

I chose 'Blowin' in the Wind', appropriately quiet and requiring no elaborate stage business, and standing there crooning, with the whole room singing along, I thought about how the villagers would react the following morning to the PowerPoint slide illustrating the thousands of spent rods we would bury beneath their floors, half a mile under the surface of the earth. They would understand. People who sing together have a positive attitude to change. You learn to listen, and adjust your tone to the tones around you. You breathe as a group. It's mainly about breathing.

Come and Play in the Milky Night

MAUREEN WAS INVOLVED in everything. She directed the North Cave Players' version of *What Anniversary*, she was a regular at American square dancing, she ran the friendship quilters' spring coffee morning, booked songstress Bobby Mandrell for the sports and social club, organised the Red Kite lecture, purchased the bluebells for the millennium walk, sourced a special cleaning solution for the war memorial, ran the shoe and handbag sale at the pub, introduced the concept of silent auctions at the WI meetings, and she had become an important mover and shaker on the parish council, having been key in getting the woman on Howden Road to cut back her bushes. Maureen was woven into the fabric of village life and even though no one knew anything about her, or exactly where she lived, or whether she had any family, we accepted her as one of our own.

The letter from East Riding District Council thanked North Cave Parish Council for its swift response to their query about the number of rough sleepers in the borough, a figure they required so they could report against a government performance indicator. However, they were not happy with North Cave Parish Council's response, which was nil. East Riding Council understood that a person was indeed sleeping rough in the parish of North Cave and the council required this situation to be investigated so that the rough sleeper could be helped to access appropriate council services. Winter was approaching and no one should be allowed to sleep rough in cold weather, especially in an area that was, after all, one of the more affluent and pleasant parts of East Riding. If it was established that there were no rough sleepers at all in the parish of North Cave, then part of the council's housing support grant could well be redirected to more so-called needy areas, like Hull.

Everyone on the Parish Council was surprised at the letter. North Cave was not the sort of place people slept rough. But they agreed it should be investigated and that night Ron Durney, leader of the Parish Council, went out with a torch and searched every hedge and every bush and every field, every barn and every outbuilding. He looked behind walls. He even looked up trees. It was a last minute decision to visit the wetlands. The wetlands were well managed and regularly patrolled by the wetlands trust staff, and there were many specimens of scientific interest, including the protected emperor dragonfly. Rough sleepers would be unwelcome.

He was shining his torch at the water's edge, disturbing a group of ducklings, when he heard foot scrapes and turned to discover Maureen walking along with a rolled up sleeping bag. She was returning from a late meeting with the environmental committee of East Riding Council where, on behalf of the Parish Council, she'd been following up on an enquiry about the North Cave road sweeping rota.

'You've caught me, Mr Durney,' she said.

They stood together in the dark, Mr Durney's torch beam playing on the edge of the water.

'Come,' she said. 'I'll tell you all about it,'

He followed her to a bench.

'Mr Durney,' said Maureen, 'I always longed to be part of a community like North Cave's. I live in a high-rise flat on the outskirts of Hull. I used to visit Howden and North Cave on a Sunday with my kids, and I used to read the village notice board about all the activities and imagine how lovely it would be to be part of such a busy, warm community. Then the kids left and I thought, why not.'

She stood up.

'I expect you'll be wanting me to leave.'

'Maureen,' Ron Durney said, 'it's not as simple as that.'

'Well, before you decide,' she said, 'come and see how nice it is where I sleep.' She took his hand and led him to a raised palette covered in straw under a tree by the water's edge. Ron helped her unroll her sleeping bag and watched her kick off her shoes and wriggle in. As it was a chilly night and there were several more issues to discuss, Ron climbed inside the bag as well. He listened to her talking about the social societies and music clubs and walking associations she was part of, and as he listened he watched the stars grow brighter over the wetlands, heard geese chuckling as they settled down to sleep, and felt the warmth of Maureen's head as it rested against his shoulder.

Acknowledgements

The author would like to thank the following for publishing and in some cases commissioning stories in this collection: Hull Literature Festival for *24 Stories*, which formed a sequence related to the M62 motorway between Liverpool and Hull, *Flash* magazine for 'Away Day', the Storey Institute and Lancaster litfest for 'Towns in France Exactly Like This', 'Buildings Crying Out', 'Domino Bones', and 'What You See Is There', Blank Pages for 'Gelling', Manchester Art Gallery and Manchester Literature Festival for 'Everlast', 'Live Feed', 'I Liked Everything', 'Portraits of Insane Women', and 'Heart Keeps Holding On', Sawn Off Opera Company for producing an operatic version of 'Are Friends Electric?', Litro for 'Spoilt Victorian Child' and others, Flax for 'Celia's Mum's Rat', *.Cent* for 'Shaky Ron and the Chewing Gum Robots', *Riptide* for 'The History Brush', 'The Three Daves', 'Remaking the Moon', 'How the Taste Gets In', and 'Come and Play in the Milk Night', Inkermen for 'Desire Lines', *Ambit* for 'Monkeys in Love' and others, and Wigan Literature Festival for 'Is Your Thought Really Necessary'. 'Not Static' appeared as 'I Won't Share You' in the anthology *Paint a Vulgar Picture, Stories Inspired by The Smiths* (Serpents Tail, ed. Peter Wild) and 'Some World Sonewhere' appeared in the collection *Punk Fiction*. Thanks also to the following for their careful reading of the manuscript and invaluable support and advice: Susan Gaffney, Mathilde Favre, Peter Wild, Nick Thompson, Socrates Adams-Florou, Tania Hershman, and Wena Poon.

DAVID GAFFNEY is from Manchester. He is the author of *Sawn Off Tales* (Salt, 2006), *Aromabingo* (Salt, 2007), *Never Never* (Tindal Street, 2008), 'Buildings Crying Out', a story using lost cat posters (Lancaster Litfest, 2009), *23 Stops To Hull*, short stories about every junction on the M62 (Humber Mouth Festival, 2009), *Destroy PowerPoint*, stories in PowerPoint format for Edinburgh Festival in August 2009, *The Poole Confessions*, stories told in a mobile confessional box (Poole Literature Festival, 2010), and has written articles for the *Guardian*, the *Sunday Times*, the *Financial Times* and *Prospect* magazine.